Josh,

I agonized a bit over personal message to you to put oneself out there .... especially to someone who has been an inspiration to follow your dreams, who doesn't even know who you are. I'm a huge fan of your work and Marianas Trench. The Astoria album cycle, however, really got my husband and I re-evaluating where we are in our lives. We'd been ~~idea for the Gate~~ WRIGHT sitting on the idea for the Gate WRIGHT trilogy for 3 years. Coming back to it off and on when our day to day jobs got too stressful or too much. I want to THANK you for unknowingly encouraging us to try our hand at what we have been dreaming of and to set an example for our kids that if you don't try you'll never know.

Stacey and Jason Warren

Thank you,

WRIGHT your own adventure!

ISBN: 1775043908
ISBN-13: 978-1775043904 (Stacey and Jason Warren)

DEDICATION

There are too many people to thank for this. Those that supported us, those that helped us and those that just listened.

In the end this book is for our girls and their dreams. It is for our mothers without whom this would not have been possible.

And for each other.

To love forever.

CHAPTER ZERO

Year: 202,437 A.L.

A dull glow revealed a pair of hands in the darkness. Fingers moved quickly over a backlit panel of complex controls, slides, and gauges. The glowing light illuminated an exhalation, a puff of warm air in the cold, though darkness masked the owner of the breath and the darting fingers. A sigh echoed in the cold room.

The sigh came again, louder and with shades of annoyance and growing frustration.

"It would be nice if you could at least give me some light," she said to the glowing panel. There was no response. "Or heat." She rubbed her hands together. "Where'd I leave that tablet?"

Her hands fumbled in the darkness, running along the edge of the control panel in search of a handle. "There we are." She pulled something from the drawer and turned it several times before finding what she was looking for. The tablet's screen powered up, bathing her face in light. She squinted. "Ah geez, what a boot up. Don't these things have a night mode?"

The shadows cast by the tablet backlighting made her look much older than she was. The long stasis she had just awakened from contributed to that effect. If she'd been able to see how unflattering and aged the tablet backlighting made her look, she'd be even more frustrated. The work was taking its toll, physically and mentally. She was tired beyond her three decades of non-stasis living. *Of course*, she reminded herself, *I am over eight thousand years old now, so I can expect a few wrinkles.*

As her sight adjusted she tapped the screen a few times, then slid two fingers slowly up the display. The ambient lighting in the room rose in tandem. She brought the virtual slider up halfway and looked up without

1

taking her hand off the screen to survey the control room she had been in every day since starting her career.

There were two seats, each with its own sleek black control panel full of buttons; only hers was occupied and currently lit. Each station had a short cabinet attached to the underside of the panel. The other workstation was a mess. Wrappers from rations littered the floor, encircled by empty drink containers. Papers stuck out of the open drawer. "Four hundred years and you can't pick up after yourself, Ben?" she said, expecting no response. "Guess picking up is going on my list of things to do this shift."

She glanced around the rest of the room to confirm there were no issues. Numerous powered-down panels lined the walls. The single entrance hatch was open and a dark expanse of hallway lay beyond.

Turning her attention back to the tablet she moved the slider down about an inch. Swiping away the environmental control, she brought up a second window with an endless stream of complex data scrolling across it. A smile formed as she read some of it; giddy excitement crept up to smooth some of the lines on her face. She exhaled. "We made it."

Reviewing more data, she added, "And within minutes of expectations. That is impressive. For all your mess, Ben, you are amazing at math." She swiped that window away and set the tablet precariously on the edge of her control panel.

"Let's see how you look," she said and flipped a button on her workstation. Several of the monitors lining the control room came online; most of them showed immense star fields extending into infinity. The screen in front of her buzzed to life a few seconds later. Her eyes had been trained in that direction and she gasped as the image took form. The screen took up nearly the entire surface of the wall and it was filled with a massive grey-gold planet brightly lit by an unseen sun. The globe slowly turned in her view and shadows of countless mountains, yawning valleys, and titanic craters slid by.

"There you are, Alex." She had thought of the planet as a friend waiting at the end of a long road. It made the work easier.

But it wasn't a friend.

It was home.

Or, more accurately, it would be home soon.

"Soon" was ten thousand years and, within the scale of time they had waited, a drop in the bucket.

"Set your clocks, everyone, she said, "we are at our journey's end. Year zero." She hit two controls and the remaining panels in the room lit up, showing graphical representations of the planet with charts, tables, and timelines.

"Time is wasting, Alex. Let's preheat the oven."

CHAPTER ONE

Journey's End Year: 19,737

The blank paper was an abyss. Hypatia glared at the empty lines, willing the words she needed into existence. Nothing.

"Having faked her way through school and studies," she blurted, "fooling the greatest academics in the history of Iskendar..." She was young—*Too young*, she thought—to be assistant to the caretaker of the Great Library. She let the next words roll off her tongue softly. "Assistant to the caretaker of the Great... caretaker of the Great Library." A smile teetered on the edges of her mouth. Hypatia attempted to rein in the giddiness, but excitement took hold in her chest. She knew she had to be every bit the respectable professional today, but this was the goal she had been striving toward since childhood. Reaching it felt like an impossible dream come true.

Hypatia cleared her throat and sat up straight. "I need to finish this bio." One of the daily papers wanted to run a story on her and, chances were, every paper on Iskendar would run the same bio.

"I'll start with looks." She was pretty enough, she figured, though not strikingly beautiful. Her skin looked soft and her eyes dark. She had pulled her vivid auburn hair up tightly on top of her head in preparation for her first day at the Great Library.

Her pen touched the paper, and a small dot of black ink slowly spread as it rested there. No words came to her and the paper remained determinedly vacant of ideas.

"I'll talk about my support network, then." She lifted the pen from the page. Encouraging and resourceful parents, the greatest teachers, friends... *Sure*, she thought. *I sacrificed a social life, fun, free time, and seeing the sun for months on end to earn it.* "What do I need friends and fun for?" she said sarcastically

3

to the wordless page taunting her with its ugly ink stain.

She knew the article was fluff. She had already made her first impression on the benefactors of the Capital. Hypatia had finished at the top of her class three years earlier than her peers. In academic circles and in casual conversation she was called The Catalogue. She admired the title. She had earned it and was proud that she was recognized for her effort.

That was the epiphany she needed. Ready with what she would write, her hand hit the page.

"Aeych!"

The shout startled her, and the words for her bio, not yet completely formed in her mind, slipped from existence. Hypatia let out an exasperated groan.

"Aeych!" Her mother had come up with a new nickname for her. It was supposed to be her first initial only, but something sounded off.

"Aeych!"

She hated it.

Her name, Hypatia Theonius of Iskendar, sounded grand and full of history. Like the title The Catalogue, it was a name she was proud of. Someday, she knew, she would be Hypatia Theonius, Caretaker of the Great Library of Iskendar. But for now...

"Aeych! You have to leave soon if you don't want to be late." Her mother had an innate sense of time, even in the darkest parts of the night, with or without the stars.

Hypatia shot a glance at the blank sheet of paper mocking her failure. The image that conjured made her laugh in spite of her disappointment. The giddiness and excitement again took hold. Her hands shot up to her mouth to muffle the escaping squeak of elation.

Rising from the writing table, she adjusted her long dress to smooth the lines along her small figure. She fumbled with the elaborate laces of her sandals. They were luxurious in comfort but a ridiculous chore to put on. Finally, giving the dress a final tug from the top, she cast the unwritten bio with its ugly black ink spot into the trash.

Her mother was setting out some juice as Hypatia entered the kitchen. She opened her mouth to speak.

"No time," Hypatia shouted, grabbing a glass of beige-coloured juice. She downed it. "Mmm, fresh sprel."

"It reminds me that the light seasons are nearly here," her mother said. "Your darling father built me a trellis for a few of the climbing vines." Hypatia's father had a thing for lattices. "They always flower the brightest when they have the room to spread out. I found the perfect place to install it along the sun side of the rear garden wall, near the roses."

Her father, Quint, came in through the patio doors, pulling off a pair of work gloves. "You should be making enough money to get your own garden soon, and your own home to go with it." Beaming with pride, he snapped his gloves in the air. "My girl, the caretaker of the Great Library."

"Assistant to the caretaker," she corrected him, grabbing his gloves from his waving hands.

"For now," he said with a wink.

"For now," Hypatia agreed, kissing him and dropping his gloves on the table. She scooped up her books and gulped down what was left of her juice before heading out.

She dashed through the garden and out the front gate. Pulling her bicycle from its slot in the stone wall, she took off.

The mostly uphill ride to the city could be considered both long and difficult, but Hypatia was accustomed to it. Driven by adrenaline and excitement, her legs pumped quickly to climb up the streets toward the central Capital area. She would arrive at the Library with a light sheen of sweat that the men of the Capital seemed to appreciate as a desirable glow. The hum of the streetlamps served as background noise in the dim glow of morning. Occasionally she saw a candle in the window of a house she zipped past.

The packed-gravel road gave way to cobblestone smoothed by centuries of use. Slowing her bike as she approached one of the more popular coffee shops in town, Hypatia waved. Gaius, who happened to be looking up while clearing a table on the shop's patio, waved back. Exciting new job or not, Hypatia could not forego her daily ritual of downing a cup of his best brew.

"Hypatia!" he shouted as he saw her, not intending it as a greeting, though it worked well for that, too.

An unseen barista acknowledged from somewhere back inside the shop, "Coming up!"

On Iskendar, like masonry and gardening, coffee was an art. Most people were involved in academic research, study, or philosophy, and anything that aided focus or wakefulness, as caffeine did, was in high demand. As an artist, and as a businessman, Gaius understood his market. Not only did he provide vast quantities of caffeine to the most academically saturated market on the planet, he also understood the varied tastes and needs of his individual customers.

Gaius drew up a chair to a waiting table and gestured for Hypatia to sit down. "Please sit, enjoy." Though the morning crowd was in full swing, he grabbed himself a chair and joined her. "How is my new favourite patron?"

Hypatia felt her cheeks warm in embarrassment, though his comment delighted her. "Now, Gaius, I am not any more important just because I got a job."

"A job?" He leaned back.

A barista appeared out of nowhere and deposited a steaming cup of coffee in front of Hypatia. The smell of the fresh coffee wafted into Hypatia's nose and she could feel herself perking up.

Gaius continued. "You didn't just get a *job*. It is oh-so much more than that."

He looked away as someone shouted, "Thanks, Gaius!" and threw a wave toward them.

Hypatia nodded in the direction of the wave and playfully jabbed Gaius in the arm. "If anyone here is important and famous, I think it's you."

"Your new job is the second most influential position in the Capital. Maybe the world." His attention was back on her, his tone now serious. "Only the Great Librarian can have more intellectual sway."

Hypatia was aware of the political weight that the Great Librarians wielded throughout the ages and was delighted to imagine she could have the same influence. She kept it to herself, but she suspected Gaius sensed her excitement. "Leaders are free to listen to and ignore any advice that comes from the Offices of Historical Study and Information," she said, attempting to downplay her excitement.

"Of course they can. At their own folly, too. Look at the last government, taken down by a policy error. The Great Librarian writes out a memo to the House and *whoosh*" —he swept his hands down in a flushing motion— "time for a new election."

"Yes, but they were in the wrong."

"They just wanted to add clocks to the schools," Gaius said.

Another customer patted him on the back and thanked him. He shook hands and insisted that he was the thankful one, for having such wonderful patrons.

"Clocks," Hypatia said in her dry and precise The Catalogue tone, as she thought of it, "unless specifically required for timing in situations where schedules or intervals need to be adhered to for safety, are to be banned— by the order of the Founders." She softened her tone. "In any case, clocks lead to bells. Bells need more complex technology. Technology is advancement. All of a sudden we are on the road to the downfall our Founders—"

Another interruption: "Thanks, Gaius!"

"Take care out there," Gaius responded.

"Our Founders were trying to save us from," Hypatia finished.

Gaius turned back to her. "Of course. But all I'm saying is, if you stand up for the government, they last. If you want it to fall, it falls."

Hypatia shrugged. "All I do is read books, share information, and help piece all of it together."

"Speaking of sharing information—" Gaius reached over to the table next to them, recently vacated. He grabbed a newspaper left next to an empty cup and laid it in front of Hypatia with a big smile. "Looks like you are the talk of the town."

She took a long sip of coffee. *Perfect*, she thought, *as always*. Without setting down her cup, she read the headline: *Great Library To Be Catalogued*. She chuckled at the play on words. She also felt a bit nervous about it, and Gaius must have sensed that.

"You earned the attention. You deserve it all—the job, the responsibility, the headlines. There isn't anyone who could do it better. Trust me, I know." As if on cue, another patron shouted a thank you as he rushed by, as did the woman who followed him. "You are most welcome. Please come again." He winked at Hypatia, who was wondering if he'd planned the speech and the interruptions, as the delivery was flawless. "The Librarian was already by here this morning; she didn't say much, but I did overhear that you would be working the night shift to start."

This didn't surprise Hypatia, but as she was considering how she might have to alter her sleep schedule and how she'd get Gaius's coffee every day, there was a shout and a crash of metal on metal on the street. She turned to look, as did everyone else on the patio.

A man in long robes, the material particularly busy around his arms and wrists, was struggling to extricate himself from a tangle of bikes and chains. "Ah, ouch," he groaned as he pushed himself to his feet.

Gaius popped up from the table and hurried over to him. "Here, let me help."

"Thank you," said the man. Hypatia recognized him as an assistant to the mayor.

Gaius grabbed the man's arm and pulled him upright. "Let me get you something, on the house. Ianto!"

"Coming up!" came the call back from inside the shop.

"Thank you again." Ianto stretched his arm out. "These robes we have to wear are getting more ridiculous by the day." He glanced toward the scene of the accident. "Oh no."

Hypatia realized in that moment that it was *her* bike he had collided with. *Oh no* could not mean anything good.

Ianto looked back and noticed Hypatia's concern. "I got caught up in the handle, and..."

"It's okay," Hypatia said in a soothing voice. "Are you alright?"

"I'm fine, but your bicycle..."

Gaius had left them and was pulling her ride from the wreckage. She could see that the chain ring was bent out of alignment. It wasn't so bad that it couldn't be fixed, but there was no way it could be fixed right now. It would need to be repaired at a shop, or perhaps even replaced.

"I am sure it will be okay. I just need to..." Remembering the distance she had to cover to get to work, Hypatia glanced up at the sky. The sun was now just peeking over the stone roof of the Great Library in the distance.

7

Without her bike, she was going to be late, unless— She knew, having been here at this time before, that she had about enough time to run ten blocks before she was due to arrive. The Library was twelve blocks away.

She started to run.

As she took off, she heard Gaius calling behind her, "Good luck! I'll stay open late—" She lost the end of his sentence as his voiced faded out behind her. She managed an awkward wave back at him as she ran.

Government buildings, offices, and monolithic buildings flew by as her sandals slapped against the cobblestones. The smells of coffee, baked goods, drying ink, and grease invaded her nostrils as she passed archways marking the entrances to bookstores, restaurants, printing presses, and repair shops. People bustled about, oblivious to The Catalogue running past. Her memory would store everything she observed.

As she ran, Hypatia catalogued all the sights and sounds of the city. She had a memorized map of the city for nearly every day she'd passed through it, each with its small differences. She could flawlessly recall each day when she focused.

Expensive clothing displays dominated a few blocks, most featuring long gowns in various light colours. The current fashion favoured a lot of pleating, abundant layers, and matching footwear. Hypatia's dress was made of a thin material that suited movement like running or cycling and would not be featured in any of the designers' stores. Most of the dresses and tops had much deeper necklines than Hypatia was comfortable with.

She suddenly realized that she had forgotten her coffee—not that her focus required it, though it did help—but that she had forgotten to pay for it. This wasn't the first time this sort of thing had happened, which was why she had a tab at Gaius's shop. She could pay for it later, but if she was going to be the most influential person in the Capital, she would have to be more professional.

Hypatia slowed as she reached the steps of the Library, certain she'd set a personal best for running. She looked up and noted that the sun was right where she'd hoped it would be. Pleased with herself, she climbed the steps to the opening below the five words carved into the stone that sent a shiver of excitement through her: *The Great Library of Iskendar.*

A nervous-looking junior Library staffer waited to one side, beside one of the two main columns flanking the entrance. He cleared his throat and held out a welcoming hand. "Congratulations, Hypatia." He cleared his throat again. "Welcome to your first day. I mean, your first day as the Assistant to the Great Librarian."

"Thank you," she replied, a little disappointed that the greeting party was just one person. Running seemed like a waste of energy for just one greeter.

She wished she still had her coffee.

CHAPTER TWO

The first time Hypatia had been to the Capital as a child, her parents had taken her to see the Great Library of Iskendar. It was the historical centre of the city and the cultural capital of the world. At seven years old, everything seemed bigger and more important. But now, as the great doors swept open in front of her, she felt like that child all over again.

The ornate carvings on the wooden doors seemed to dance in the electric light of the Library, casting their shadows in the deep red stain of the door panels as the junior staffer swung them open and then stood to one side, looking nervous.

Hypatia looked at him and thought, *Do I have that impact on people now?* She brushed the thought away, choosing instead to believe this was likely his first day as well. Despite her dismissal, the thought of being venerated gave her stride a confidence that she normally reserved for award receptions (those receptions where she was the recipient) as she entered the Library.

The winds of confidence were ripped from her sails as she cleared the atrium and entered into the heart of the building. A huge window, six stories high, opened onto the Capital below in a sweeping, breathtaking panorama. Hypatia walked forward and grabbed the railing. Her hands were trembling and she hoped her grip would hide her display of nerves. They were on the third floor and, looking out, she saw the endless shelves that lined every level, six floors in all. The shelves continued back into each floor, out of sight, and were populated with so many books that Hypatia imagined them overflowing in a tidal wave capable of drowning thousands. Each floor encircled the huge central room, breaking only at the edge of the great window. Warm spring sunshine poured in to illuminate the interior from the lowest level to the vaulted ceiling.

They started down the stairs. The staircase on each level was designed to look as if it grew out of the floor below it, sweeping upward organically. The flickering shadows cast by electric candlelight made them appear alive.

At the apex of the ceiling hung a chandelier sporting thousands of the same faux candles; far below it, a long table constructed from a single slab of wood rested in the middle of the open space on the lowermost floor. The table was stained the same deep red as the Library's doors and had been smoothed to a brilliance that reflected the sun shining through the Library's massive window. Though the table could easily hold fifty people, currently only a single person sat at the head of the table.

"The Librarian awaits your arrival," the junior staffer chirped, having noticed Hypatia's gaze resting on the table below. She must have looked lost in reverie, because the junior staffer placed a tentative hand on her shoulder to get her attention.

They continued the descent down the stairs. Afraid she would fall in her attempt to descend gracefully, Hypatia wished she could use one of the Library's hidden electrical lifts just this once.

As they got closer, Hypatia could see that the Librarian had a small scroll unfurled on the table before her, with a very ornate pen sitting in front of her. She was immediately impressed—the pen was made from a laceae, a flower unique to her home city of Attica. *I'll mention that,* she thought, seeking somewhere to start the conversation.

The Librarian looked up as she and the junior staffer stopped at the far end of the table. "Good morning, Hypatia."

"Good morning, uh..." It occurred to Hypatia as she stumbled that she didn't know how to address the Librarian; *Good morning, Kaelljuna Tatianus of Uskana and Great Librarian of Iskendar* sounded ridiculous in her head.

"You can call me Kalli. No need for you to be formal." She spoke in a stern but unaggressive tone—authority without pressure.

"Good morning, Kalli. That feels a bit awkward, with you being the holder of such great responsibility and influence and being so important." She knew she was babbling, but the nervousness was in control. *Sort of in control,* she thought.

"Come. Sit."

Hypatia walked the length of the table. The junior staffer scurried ahead and pulled a chair out for her, then slid it back in as she took her seat.

"Thank you, Valens. That will be all," said Kalli.

The staffer nodded. "Yes, thank you." He walked to the end of the table, stopped, and turned around to stand at attention.

Kalli watched him for a moment. "I'm sure you can find something to do, Valens." She used that same authoritative tone. It made Hypatia feel like no order was being delivered, but challenging it would make no sense. In a single breath the Librarian was providing a directive that he could choose to ignore while insisting he choose not to.

Valens nodded again and walked away down one of the many aisles that lined the first floor. Kalli turned back to Hypatia when he had finally disappeared from sight and said in a softer tone, "I don't like all the pomp and parade that goes along with these official appointments."

The Librarian carried her age well. Hypatia knew she was in her seventy-sixth year and her face showed her age, its creases revealing endless hours spent in thought. The few grey and white strands streaking her thick, dark brown hair made her look regal and experienced. She was dressed formally, but her look also leaned on comfort over style.

"There will be ample opportunity for welcoming, back patting, and parties. Today we do the paperwork." She gestured to the pen and parchment on the table. "We chat. Then I put you to work. And I am very anxious to see The Catalogue at work."

The way she said "The Catalogue" made Hypatia flush—a sensational nickname paired with a professional role seemed ridiculous. She hid her embarrassment by reaching for the pen and burying her face in the form. It was typical of many agreements she had signed before. And it was boring. Identification here—name, address, date of birth, and so on. She'd thought that somehow, this would be more exciting. It was still a job, she reminded herself, requiring all of the standard details.

She signed the last line in large looping letters and slid the form over to the Librarian, who reviewed it slowly.

"Just twenty-three?" Kalli said. "My goodness, so young."

"Some say you were the youngest Great Librarian to ever grace Iskendar," Hypatia said, recalling that Kalli had been the Librarian for over fifty years, "And yet here you are, one of the most revered figures in the world."

"My girl, humanity is quite likely millions of years old. I don't mention your age because your youth makes you incapable of the job. Word of your ability, your memory, and your intelligence precedes you. There has not been enough time, in twenty-three years, to absorb all of this." She waved her hand at the stacks and Hypatia could not help being impressed again at the sight. "There is so much to know and so little time to know even a small part of it."

Hypatia's heart fluttered as she took it all in.

Kalli gestured and the junior staffer, Valens, who had retreated to the stacks, appeared on cue from an aisle behind the Librarian. Hypatia guessed he must have made his way along the outer wall of the first floor and took up position closer, waiting for the call. She handed Hypatia's file to him and gestured to the pen and inkwell. "Thank you. That will be all."

He hastily scooped up the writing tools, inadvertently spilling some ink on his layered shirt. Hypatia heard the Librarian sigh as he disappeared up the stairs and out of sight.

"He is very eager, at least." Turning her attention to Hypatia, she continued. "And I imagine you are, as well. Today I'd like you to familiarize yourself with the archives of the Founders." Hypatia shifted in her seat. "Not the sealed archives, though. There is training you must have before we allow you access to those, as the documents are very fragile. Especially when handled by someone as excited as you on your first day. Preparation . . ." She trailed off in thought.

"Preparation?"

"Yes." Kalli stood and continued in a slow, calculated voice. "That is all I will say for now. The mayor will be looking to meet with you later today. As such, he has scheduled an appointment. He already has some ideas for a rousing speech" —she said "rousing" with a sigh similar to the one Valens had received— "to formally introduce you to the public. The words of the Founders are always crowd-pleasing in the Capital. You will want to have done some fresh reading in advance of the discussion. Are you okay with that?"

Hypatia loved to study the Founders. "Oh yes," she blurted. "The Founders are just fascinating. Ten thousand years since their landing and there is still so much we need to learn. To understand."

"I am aware of the specifics. As you may have guessed, I have some experience with the knowledge kept within these walls. There are many things here that you will not have learned elsewhere. Some information is not made available to all communities. I suspect, despite your— reputation—you will have questions. I'd recommend you start with Ageis."

"Because of his detailed documentation of the last remnants of the Founders?"

"No, because his name starts with *A*." She smiled. "You will find our version of his work more complete than others. I expect you need no direction to find it."

Hypatia did not.

Heading toward the stairs, Kalli added, "We will meet shortly before lunch to discuss what the mayor has planned for your meeting." Then she moved quickly up the steps with more efficiency than grace.

Pleased with how her first exchange with her new boss had gone, Hypatia nearly bounded down the aisles, taking a scenic route through the stacks to soak in the titles as she passed. Most of the contents of the books she passed were already stored in Hypatia's Catalogue memory. As she read the titles she recalled passages relevant to each.

Seeing *Building a Capital*, she thought: *Agriculture is the strength of a community but discourse is the heart.*

On a lower shelf, *Revolution of the Third Age* produced: *The harder the road is to traverse, the more valuable the treasure it yields.*

It was the better part of an hour before Hypatia reached the section dedicated to the Founders. It had no significant markers other than the numerical identification used to denote this collection: Section One. With little thought she knew where *The Artifacts of Arcadia* would be. Ageis had a significant space dedicated to his work and *The Artifacts* was his most well known. The *Arcadia* was the ship that had carried the Arcadians, the last bastion of humanity, to Iskendar. They established the first colonies that produced the generation of the Founders.

She pulled it from the shelf and noted how much thicker this volume was compared to hers. Hypatia had to carry it with two hands. Seeing the physical difference, feeling the weight of it, excited Hypatia. She thought of the new knowledge and the new insights she would gain and, if she was being honest with herself, felt a little smug in knowing more than others about a subject.

She took the book back to the large table in the central atrium. It thumped down loudly on the heavy wood. She looked up to see if anyone heard. If they had, no one looked. *It would be nice to be noticed, now that I'm the assistant*, she thought. Slightly disappointed, she sat down and took out a pen and paper. Opening to her favourite part, she started reading.

The Founders had basic manuals for farming, forestry, and masonry as well as medical salves, powders, and the detailed instructions to recreate them. The remaining records . . .

Remaining records? she thought. This was new.

The remaining records recovered from the Arcadia were stored in a panel no thicker than the width of one finger. The panel would glow as if a lamp were stored inside.

The Founders used electricity? She felt her skin tingling with the new knowledge. Hypatia was having a revelation on her first day of work and the world needed to know about it. This book was out in the open for everyone. *It must have been read a thousand times before, though*, she thought. *Every other version must have had this intentionally omitted.*

Her excitement dwindled. The Librarian would know and had directed her to this for that specific reason. She shelved what remained of her eagerness at the discovery and, returning to the calm that The Catalogue was known for, turned her attention back to *The Artifacts*.

The knowledge of the tablet's functions was held by the remaining descendants that exited the Arcadia. Stories were secretly told, about how to use the technology long ago abandoned by the Arcadians. It is believed that this resource held a million books and a billion pages of history, science, and art predating the Arcadia itself.

Hypatia released a breath she hadn't realized she was holding in. All the knowledge of their history before Iskendar was stored in something smaller than a few pages. She was having difficulty comprehending the technology that allowed it.

The morning passed with more revelations but was marked with far more repetition and familiarity than this.

Her second meeting with the Great Librarian, arriving more quickly than she had expected, boiled down to Hypatia delivering a summary of the revelations she had discovered. Kalli confirmed that there had been deliberate editing.

"Maybe I could anchor my speech as assistant around lifting the veil on knowledge."

"It does fit with your reputation as 'The Catalogue.' Details are messy." Kalli was clearly thinking on it. "Details are critically important for proper evaluation. Messy, though." She left it at that. "You are to meet with Oren this afternoon." Kalli stood on this note, swiftly ending the conversation and sending Hypatia off to the office of the mayor. "I do not expect to see you until tomorrow. Night," she had said at last as she closed the meeting.

Hypatia needed no additional details. She was already well aware of the night routine of the Library. She understood she was to oversee the activities of the few night patrons. Of course, she would be expected to carry out her studies in that same shift.

She left the Library, tipping her head back as she stepped into the bright midday sun. She would be unlikely to see sunlight again for the next few weeks.

CHAPTER THREE

When Hypatia arrived at the office of the mayor, the assistant-to-an-administrator-of-the-official-keeper-of-the-mayor's-timetable greeted her and asked her to wait in an adjoining meeting room. Other people came and went through the big doors that marked the entrance to the inner sanctum of the elected head of the Capital.

Hypatia retreated into her thoughts, sorting how she might introduce herself with the mayor and, more formally, to the Capital.

The assistant reappeared some time later, after Hypatia had revised her speech and her presentation several times in her head. She'd also been able to add a post-dinner celebration. He was sorry for the delay but made it clear that "the government is always hard at work." He disappeared again before she could respond. *Hardly justification*, Hypatia thought.

Before her next update, Hypatia had had enough time to further perfect the speech and the presentation, determine a menu for a twelve-course celebration dinner, plan a musical playlist for the dance that was sure to follow, and had begun scripting all the custom thank-you notes for the hundreds of important attendees. This time she was greeted by a different assistant-to-the-administrator-of-the-official-meeting-planner-of-the-city
and asked to wait in a different adjoining meeting room. Taking it in stride, Hypatia changed meeting rooms.

She was almost clear into planning her retirement after a life's work when, finally, the administrator she had met when she first arrived returned and let her know that she was to make her appearance in the mayor's office. After the achingly long delay, she was now hurried past a large reception area and through a pair of grand marble doors.

"Hypatia!" Mayor Oren exclaimed, loud enough to surprise Hypatia as she entered. "Come in! Come in!" He popped up from his desk, extending his hand and moving briskly across the expanse of stone floor to meet her at the entrance of the cavernous domed office.

As she shook his hand she noticed the desk was flanked by six benches. In front of each bench stood two members of what Hypatia assumed was his cabinet, or maybe the cabinet members' assistants. She recognized a few. Etrius had voted for her appointment and made his choice very public. Beside him was Demeter, who had been just as public about his opposing opinion. As a group, though, they showed excitement in her arrival. Demeter began clapping, which launched a spattering of applause from the other eleven. The mayor let go of her hand and began applauding as well.

"Greetings and congratulations from the Capital. We are excited to begin work on building a new, healthy, and refreshed Iskendar and you are integral in this revolution," Oren said as he led her to a bench in the centre of the room. "As you know, it has been decades since a new Assistant to the Great Librarian was appointed." The stone bench was ornately carved and overflowing with cushions and freshly cut floral decoration. Sitting might present some difficulty, Hypatia thought.

She was sizing up the bench when Etrius approached her. He greeted her, thanked her for her work, and retreated to his bench. Demeter followed, and then the others each greeted her personally. They gave their name, title, and how excited\thankful\impressed they were to meet\work with\talk to her. Hypatia answered each with her best professional-sounding response, attempting to show no favour or disappointment with anyone.

Once each dignitary had greeted her and returned to their appointed place she sat, delicately, on her own bench. Several cushions slid imperceptibly and, as if she had planned it, two blue petals fell from flowers on each side of her. With a tremendous amount of collecting up garments, shuffling pillows, and interpersonal chatter, everyone else sat as well.

Oren called them to order in his usual enthusiastic tone, then addressed Hypatia. "Thank you for coming to our small symposium today. It is wonderful to greet the next Great Librarian." Another outburst of clapping, excited exchanges, and congratulations. "We will be holding a gala celebration of your appointment in two weeks' time."

Someone started to clap again but Oren held up his hand. "No more applause. If we keep that up, it will take until sun rising to get through all of this."

"Sounds like one of your election speeches," one of the middle-aged cabinet ministers said loudly, earning general laughter.

"Quite." Oren threw an annoyed glance at the minister who had spoken. "Let us keep the humour and congratulations to a minimum."

Hypatia was smiling. She had expected them to be professional, boring, and uptight. This chaos was an entertaining surprise.

"Your speech," the mayor began. He was standing now and as he spoke, he strutted about the room, waving his arms. This was Oren in his element: delivering an argument to the floor and not specifically speaking to Hypatia. "As you will be required to give a speech, you will reflect upon this cabinet and the government of the Capital as a whole. You would, of course, expect this to set a precedent for our direction. We, the governing authority who could be considered the heart of the Capital, must be seen as acting in coordination with the centre of intellectualism and study, which could be considered the mind of the Capital."

The metaphor was clearly well rehearsed. It intrigued Hypatia. It suggested to her that the government was incapable of thought—not a new assessment of politicians. She laughed a little and said, "And so must the body or the people of the Capital act in response to the heart and the mind."

It wasn't rude in the Capital to interrupt an orator if the speaker was skilled in doing so. Hypatia was an expert. She was regarded as such, and to be interrupted by her input was a blessing to most speakers.

"Of course!" Emboldened by her support, Oren somehow managed to increase the vigour and conviction of his speech. "Your youth. Your knowledge. Your love for the Founders' beliefs. You demonstrate these characteristics in both reputation and practice. We desire that you imbue your presentation with those things that make you so renowned. Highlight change and growth. Temper it, though, by celebrating the legacies that have so successfully carried Iskendar for ten thousand years."

He really isn't saying anything definite, Hypatia thought. Her ideas were at the ready, on the tip of her tongue, formed perfectly in her mind. Oren did not provide another opportunity for interruption. His speech continued for another half hour as it had started, mixing obvious clichés, pointless dichotomies, and grand emotional posturings about histories and peoples.

As he appeared to be nearing some conclusion, Oren knelt before Hypatia, his head bowed. "I speak for all of us when I say" —he dramatically lifted his face to look at her— "thank you, Hypatia. Good luck." He rose to his feet, pulling Hypatia to her feet with him. "And welcome, our future Great Librarian!" He turned, presenting her to the ministers of the cabinet.

They rose from their seats, also with great drama, and there was a flurry of applause and back patting. Hypatia was shaking hands again, hearing "thank you" and "good luck" as she was ushered from the mayor's hall.

She suddenly found herself standing in the lobby, alone. "Well that was useless."

Leaving the government building, she headed home. A long walk and a warm night unfolded before her. As she came up her road, her footfalls made little noise as they kicked up little clouds of dust, visible in the light of the electric lamps.

17

Sitting outside her house, tucked into its usual slot in the low stone wall, was her bicycle.

That was nice of Gaius to return it, she thought. As she got closer, she noticed that the chain was no longer broken. There was a new chain, and the handles had been readjusted. The bicycle had even received a fresh paint job. It looked brand new.

Hypatia admired it for a moment before she strode up the walkway through the garden with a confident air. She was excited about the attention he was giving her. The cost of the repairs was easily more than she spent on coffee in a month. Not to mention the time he must have taken off to get it done. Maybe Gaius was trying to win her over.

Hypatia hadn't thought much about romance or relationships for most of her life. It wasn't that she'd never considered it—she had. She had even thought about Gaius as an attractive, well-off suitor. "Not to mention all the free coffee." She laughed to herself.

"Something funny?" Her father had been sitting by the reflecting pool with a book open in his lap. He looked up at her as she circled around from the garden entrance. "And what's this about free coffee?"

Quint was a coffee addict. Their whole family and even the neighbours knew how much he loved his daily fix. He would be gardening, dust, dirt, and organic matter flying, and at regular intervals he'd reach over for his cup of coffee. The neighbours would laugh and call out, "Get some dirt in there, Quint?" and he'd smile, lift his cup, make a joke about natural flavours, and take a sip. If her father knew about Gaius's interest, he would be as happy as a dog in a dirt pile.

A huge smile grew on his face. Dog, meet dirt pile. He knew. "I see a certain well-regarded shop owner personally delivered your bike—looking brand new, I might add—while you were gone."

"I noticed." Suddenly uncharacteristically bashful, she had to raise her hand to stifle a smile before her father noticed.

"He did appear quite crestfallen when I told him a certain well-regarded lady was not at home."

"I'm sure you just imagined that." She sat down with him on the stone bench.

"Hmm, maybe." He kept the grin on his face. "But he made it very clear I was to mention that he would keep the shop open late for you on your first night shift. With your favourite order waiting."

"He stays open late on a good many nights. Lots of people stop there when working late and a lot of people work late in the Capital. Coffee is a big seller."

"Possibly. Does Gaius make personal visits to all of his patrons' homes with freshly painted bicycles and crestfallen disappointment? That seems an expensive and emotionally taxing way to run a coffee shop."

"Oh, Dad." She pushed him with the ferocity a daughter reserves for embarrassing fathers. "You are just hoping and dreaming for free unlimited coffee."

"That does sound nice." He sipped at a coffee he pulled from a stone drink holder that was a perfect fit for his mug. "Maybe I'll marry him."

Hypatia rose. "I don't think your wife would approve."

He laughed a deep laugh that was full of pride, excitement, and life. No wonder, Hypatia thought; things were exactly as a father might dream of: a happy marriage, a successful daughter, and a coffee baron for a potential son-in-law. His laughter made her feel warm.

She felt home.

CHAPTER FOUR

The stars sparkled against the blue-black sky. The mountains silhouetted on the horizon looked as if they held back the endless universe from swallowing the world whole. Iskendar spun slowly, but Hypatia felt she was able to perceive the map of the stars spinning before her. She knew the locations of the stars so well that, with her eyes closed, she could point within a reasonable margin of error to where any star would be.

On this night Hypatia felt like she was seeing the sky with new eyes. A page had turned and everything was different.

The sun had barely set when she awoke. She was surprised that she'd been able to get a decent amount of sleep, despite her anticipation of her first night at the Library. She dressed and made her way to the kitchen, where she was surprised again by the dinner her mother had waiting. It was a cold supper of flatbread, fresh fruits, some pickled vegetables, and more of the sprel juice. She ate quietly, planning her evening's study by mapping out in her mind the path she would take to all the relevant locations in the Library.

Her mother and father were snuffing out the candles from their nearly ritualistic evening respite in the garden when she stepped out of the house. On most nights Hypatia would look forward to joining them, and she felt a twinge of loneliness as she wished them good night and left. Pushing the feeling from her mind, she let The Catalogue take over.

For the inaugural address, she planned to talk about the fragments of history that were taught. Hypatia now knew there was so much more than the tailored teachings of the mass-produced textbooks, and the new Assistant to the Great Librarian would be the light to shine on that shadow.

"What will be learned when everyone knows?" she wondered aloud as she walked. "What insights will we gain? Why was it hidden?" The "why" was even more interesting than the "what" for Hypatia.

Staring up at the stars, lost in her thoughts of altered and redacted histories, Hypatia paid no attention to her surroundings and those who greeted her as she walked—until the complex aromas of freshly brewed coffee snapped her out of her philosophizing.

"Good evening, Hypatia."

Gaius stood in front of the darkened café, the patio devoid of the life and bustle that charged it during the previous day. Hypatia wasn't used to seeing it so empty and quiet.

"I closed early," he said as he extended a fresh cup of coffee toward her. The steam escaped from a small opening in the lid and disappeared into the cool night.

Thanking him, she accepted the cup and noticed he had one of his own. Gaius raised it to his mouth for a sip, took stock of the steam escaping, and thought better of it. "Mind if I escort you?" he asked as he blew cool air across the lid.

"Escort me? How formal, Gaius. I'm just on my way to work."

"All the more reason for formality. As a professional courtesy, a proud but humble small business owner would be honoured if you, the Assistant to the Great Librarian, would accept his offer of an" —he held out his hand— "escort."

She laughed and, feigning stiff formality, replied, "Why, of course dear, proud—"

"And humble," he interjected.

"Yes, and humble business—"

"And funny."

"And funny," she added.

"And gorgeous."

Taking his arm, smiling, she said, "And passably attractive small business owner."

"I'll take that." He smiled back at her.

They walked toward the city centre chatting, laughing occasionally, and touching each other lightly in appreciation of a good joke or a shared compliment. To anyone passing by it was evident that far more than a friendship was on display.

Nearly all of the shops had closed. While the streets were still busy with groups of people socializing or milling about, no one seemed pressed to be anywhere. Music, conversation, and bursts of loud, raucous laughter drifted down alleyways from distant parties, and out the windows above the shops.

It had occurred to Hypatia that Gaius had been waiting for her even though she had left early for her scheduled shift. The coffee was still hot when she arrived. Gaius would have known when she started, but how did he know she'd be early? Was she so predictable? She studied him, attempting to read his thoughts, and wondered if she should ask him about her banality. Gaius, oblivious to his own surroundings as he often was when talking, was heatedly explaining recent news in the relationships of two well-known and politically powerful couples. Tawdry rumours of infidelity and subterfuge were always juicy topics on Iskendar.

He stopped talking, noticing her staring at him, and smiled, warmth and openness emanating from his whole body. He had wide, watery grey eyes that invited secrets, confessions, and rumours from many different sources. She could understand why. She wanted to share everything she knew with him too.

His hair, while thinning, was an organized mess on his head. It didn't hide the fact that he was balding (a common trait in the Capital), but it kept his appearance playfully youthful.

Gaius caught her sizing up his hair. "My balding is premature. I am quite young still."

"I know. It suits you though, Gaius. That young and—"

"And gorgeous."

"Ahem," she cut back in. "And handsome face is deceptively innocent. You know a lot more that you let on. People share their secrets with you and you keep the important ones to yourself. I think you use that to your café's benefit. The right secrets can be quite powerful, and I think your hair can't take the stress of it." She allowed a playful smile.

"I beg to differ. I think my hair is keen to escape a sinking ship. Better to get out now than to wait for work, stress, and fatigue to ruin the rest of this." He swept his hand across his body.

"You are fishing for compliments now. I think, if you are looking to win me over, you should be providing instead of baiting."

Gaius knew an invitation when he heard it. He didn't hesitate even a moment. "Well, you are beautiful, funny, fierce, and the smartest person on Iskendar, Hypatia. I am afraid that a compliment from me would be but a drop in a sea of praise already directed at your shores."

She felt her face heat. "Well done. You do have a way with words."

"And you have a way with hearts. With one specifically."

"Now, now. That goes too far," she said as she stopped walking and turned to look into his eyes. "Coffee is nice, and the sugar is very sweet, but it is too soon for promises."

He nodded once and bent his knee slightly. "For another night, then."

"That sounds fair enough."

They continued walking the remaining distance to the Library. At the bottom of the stairs she thanked him again, and he wished her luck. The light mood in which he had offered that coffee had dimmed.

"You know, Gaius, I'd appreciate another escort, if you were open to it. It is nice for someone so important to be seen with someone so . . . gorgeous."

"I would be." He smiled, and there was a glint in his eye.

There it is, she thought.

Her first night at the Library was uneventful. Hypatia loved every moment of it, spending the entire night poring over books and filing every word she read into her catalogue. She could have done the comparisons she had planned without her personal volumes in tow, but the huge number of omissions in her own versions when compared against those in the Library made her question even her own memory. It was a new feeling for Hypatia; not trusting her memory was like not knowing if her hand could hold a pen.

And she wrote. And edited. And rewrote. This speech would define her early work and public image. She was intent on producing the speech that defined her life. It was a lot of pressure.

Her first week seemed endless. Sleeping during the day was harder than she'd expected, and the darkness and odd warmth in the Library presented a difficulty of its own, inviting Hypatia to sleep. The highlight of each day was the coffee and the walk with Gaius before every shift. He didn't always close the café, but he always escorted her to work, regaling her with the latest rumours and secrets.

On the night marking the end of her first week, with midnight long past and slumber threatening to pounce, Hypatia yawned without bothering to cover her mouth and looked up from the book she was studying. She was seated in her preferred place at the large meeting table in the main atrium, which afforded the most impressive view of the night sky. Neither of Iskendar's moons could be seen and the stars were specks of dim dust on the sky. The only light came from the covered electric lamps illuminating the floors above her.

Hypatia could make out two or perhaps three flickers between the rows of books above. She knew all of the Library departments and she envisioned the directory to the different sections in her memory. One light on the third balcony: Mathematics. *He must be cramming for something*, Hypatia thought. She swept her gaze across the open expanse above the central lobby and down one level. Second floor, near the back: Political Biographies. *A speechwriter for some rising representative of the people, to be working this late.* The third light was up far enough that she wasn't sure which section it was. She squinted. Five floors up, maybe. Fiction. Romantic fiction.

Iskendar was focused on philosophy, discussion, and intellectualism, and it was that deep well from which they drew their passion. Romance, fantasy, and art extended outward from those ideals. To describe the beauty of a flower intellectually was a layered, complex, and intricate exercise. Hypatia called to mind a passage from a popular risqué novel:

Surface of lust and desire, a flower is perfection in appearance, delicate to touch, and enticing. An overwhelming perfume. Life tempting water from the earth, endlessly reaching for another sip, another drop. A flower recoils from the dry cold of the night to unfold in the warm radiance of sunrise. With every breath the flower draws, fire chains the heat of the sun with the cold water of the earth, unwillingly, in chemical reaction. Sweet sugar released. Silent sighs of life-giving oxygen.

She didn't know why, but she was nervous.

Hypatia found herself rising from the table, abandoning her candle to move beyond its flickering light. The movement of shadows danced up the stairs, impressing upon Hypatia that she was leaving her star, a dim lamp, a universe away.

She passed by the landing on the second floor and the speechwriter, who was flipping through a small book, glanced up. For a second he thought the Library was haunted, as all libraries are, but he was too busy to worry about it.

A struggling mathematics undergraduate on the third floor uttered a squeak of surprise as she spotted a woman in white ascending past the landing.

Hypatia climbed without noticing the other patrons, scaling each carpeted stair with a quiet urgency she did not understand. Her heartbeat increased in time with each step. She had been gaining speed until, halfway up the next staircase, she stopped.

Light was dancing down the aisle. It was different, though. This was not a Library– certified covered candle. It skipped and twisted between the novels like a wild creature. Book jackets depicting passionately clasped lovers flashed into view and were swept away by shadows.

Hypatia could hear her heart pounding in her ears and feel her chest struggling to keep time with her need to breathe. It felt like pages in a book slipping from her fingers, and she could hear them.

No, she thought, *I hear pages turning.*

Whoever was here was rifling through pages unbelievably fast. She heard a book drop to the floor. Another book pulled from the shelf. More pages turning. Again and again it repeated.

She moved slowly and almost silently to the landing, until she was swallowed by the darkness of the fourth floor, then silently drifted down the aisle behind the stranger. She slid aside *The Verdant Thorn* (a hooded man grasping a woman in one arm and a bow in the other hand on the cover), and peeked through a space between some of the racier romances.

His face was in a book. He had stopped flipping and was intent on something.

From this perspective she could tell he had dark hair, full but loose, as if he'd just escaped a fierce windstorm. His hands, clasping the book, appeared equally rough. In fact, his whole look suggested "thank goodness I found my way out of the desert, those sandstorms can be brutal." His shirt was a light material that, at some point, had been a much lighter colour than it was now. The sleeves were half pushed, half rolled up his dark arms. He wore thick canvas pants that had seen better days, and boots that were only suitable for construction work.

Craning farther forward to get a view of his face, Hypatia accidentally pushed on the stack and *The Verdant Thorn* spilled to the floor in the other aisle. The stranger stopped flipping pages and slowly looked up.

His face was hard, the skin leathery. It appeared he hadn't shaved in days, but wasn't actually entertaining the idea of a beard.

He turned his head toward where the book had fallen and Hypatia instinctively swung back from her vantage point. She grabbed at her chest and covered her mouth to stifle any noise. She stood as still as possible, but the stranger wasn't making any sound.

"Come here."

Hypatia didn't move.

"I know you're there."

She heard him take a step and reach down to pick something up.

"Interesting taste in books you have. From what I've seen, this stuff is a little outside of your comfort zone."

Hypatia blurted out, "I'll have you know that I believe that diversity is a banquet for the mind." She thought for a moment that maybe she should have waited until she knew what *The Verdant Thorn* was about before she made such a bold statement of preference.

"The sun is coming up and I need to be going shortly," he said, and dropped the book to the floor. "You'll want to see this. This is the impressive part."

He's right, she thought. The sun was rising, its warm light pushing back the black of the night.

The Assistant to the Great Librarian, not quite The Catalogue but an authoritative part of Hypatia, kicked in. *Why am I afraid? This is MY library and he is the one up to—well, up to something*, she thought. Standing up straight, she pressed down her dress and then her hair with one commanding hand, and strode sternly to the end of the aisle and around to the next aisle.

The stranger was staring at her. She could see the sun cresting in his infinite indigo eyes, like a redeeming dawn following an ocean storm. Smiling faintly, he pulled a leather-bound book from behind his back. He flipped apart the straps and the book fell open, as if marked, to the required page.

He muttered something to himself. Hypatia could only make out a few words, but she didn't think they were English; it was a language she had never heard. She was going to say "Pardon?" but as her mouth opened, a gust of wind tore past her with a noise like the turning of a million pages at once.

Hypatia closed her eyes as the noise and wind overtook her. The sound grew louder as it spun around her. It filled the Library and echoed off the shelves and walls. She heard the glass of the great window rattle. Raising her arm to shield her face, she opened her eyes to see what was happening.

The space where the stranger had been standing seemed to be slicing apart and flattening into a singularity. A bright line stretched upward as fast as it closed inward, the sound pushing the limits of what she could bear. The stranger was no longer visible.

CRACK.

The wind stopped dead and there was silence.

Hypatia stood before an aisle littered with books, *The Verdant Thorn* lying atop the pile.

The stranger was gone.

CHAPTER FIVE

Sleep did not come easily the following day.

Without a word, Hypatia slipped into her room when she got home, and climbed into bed. But her mind drifted back to the encounter with the stranger and she lay awake, trying unsuccessfully to reconcile what she had seen with her understanding of the universe.

Who was he? How did he do that? Where did he come from? Was it real?

Eventually exhaustion delivered her to sleep, where the stranger invaded her dreams.

A long, hard walk took her back to the Library the next night. Gaius was away on business and she was on her own for the first time since beginning at her new position. Hypatia welcomed the solo trek, as she needed time to process what had happened before telling anyone. Gaius would have gotten the details from her no matter what stage of comfort she felt in understanding it. *Would he think I'm crazy?* she wondered. *Am I?*

Twilight softened into a long night and Hypatia's nervousness grew as darkness fell. Questions and images continued to plague her. Would the stranger be back?

Sitting down to a long night of work, she pictured him in her mind. His thick hair was ragged and loose, with no style. It must have grown from a completely shaven scalp into its current unkempt mess, she thought. Wind-tossed. Free. She absently turned a page. The thick canvas pants he wore had been tailored to fit his body. The material was heavily worn and frequently repaired; she could tell that from the tracks of holes, the ghosts of past stitches where the thread had been removed and restitched for a new size multiple times. The creases faded into white where the pants had been let out to suit his muscular legs.

She turned another page. The creases on his face were deeper than those in his overworked clothes. The shadows had traced the paths along his

27

forehead and the lines radiating from the corners of his eyes. They carved lines in his cheeks on either side of his mouth. All those lines seemed to pull her gaze into his eyes. Those eyes pierced her own until it felt like he could climb around inside her head, sorting the deeds and secrets and drawing forth anything he could want about her.

Another page turned and again she pictured him.

Sometimes, Hypatia thought, this memory, with the perfect clarity of recollection, was a terrible distraction. Two nights until the inaugural speech, and she had spent half of her time remembering, fantasizing, and wishing about the stranger.

She turned the page of the book she was studying, realized she hadn't actually read anything, and flipped back.

It was first ruled as . . .

Lightly touching her face, his hands felt calloused but warm. He traced her jawline with his fingers, the dryness of his skin making nearly imperceptible scratching sounds as they moved slowly to her chin. He tilted her face upward. Gently. *Oh, so gently.*

She was staring into his eyes. His hands brushed her lips and moved to her cheeks. His eyes were drawing closer. Was she moving, or was he? They were burrowing into her soul. Seeking all her secrets. Chains fell away, in her mind's eye, as she tried to let him in. Everything she knew was there, surfacing. His lips pressed against hers . . .

Hypatia turned the page. Then, realizing she hadn't read past the first sentence again, she swore and flipped back.

The night continued uneventfully in this way. Hypatia found herself in the romantic fiction section many times, peeking in to see if anything had changed or been disturbed, even minutely. She flipped through the same books, trying to figure out what the stranger had been searching for. She had even stood in the aisle adjacent, where she had concealed herself the night before to sneak a look between the stacks. *The Verdant Thorn* was still solidly in place.

He didn't return.

The sun rose and Hypatia packed up her books and her speech and headed home.

Gaius called out as she was heading down the hill against the busy morning foot traffic heading back into the Capital after a night's rest.

"Great morning, Hypatia."

"Morning." She smiled at him weakly. She was disappointed, but she was struggling with her own confusion as well.

"Long night?"

"Yes. I guess . . . " Suddenly guilt crept in and she stared off into another direction, past Gaius. "Glad to be done. I'm, uh, ready for a rest."

"I know what that's like," he said, not appearing to notice her distraction. "Is there anything I can do for you? Need something small for the road? I have a tea that can steal you off to dreamland and I have heard it also provides the most comforting dreams."

"Not today, Gaius. I think I might prefer dreamless, deep, and rejuvenating sleep today."

"I can understand that. Maybe I could give you a walk home?"

Her guilt subsided a little. After all, the stranger wasn't coming back. *Is he?* "I'd like that." She looked around at how busy the café was. Patrons rushed in and out as baristas whipped up drinks, clinked dishes, and wiped up tables. "If you can spare the time."

"This place runs itself." He quickly pulled off his apron and dumped it on a recently vacated patio chair. "I'll be back shortly!" he called out to the staff.

"Not too shortly, I hope!" a voice called from inside the café.

Gaius blushed at this and Hypatia, sensing his awkwardness, forgot what remaining guilt she had and took his arm as he led the way.

"Sorry for that." He was still red. It had spread from his cheeks, taking up residence in his ears, too.

"Don't be sorry. I am flattered." She pulled his arm in closer and took his hand.

CHAPTER SIX

Hypatia's progress in perfecting her speech flew along, the next night in the Great Library. She was in full revision mode, reading and rereading, with tiny tweaks made each time. *Maybe that's too much*, she'd think, and the tweak was removed for the next reading.

As a long night of work dragged into the small hours of the morning, Hypatia fell asleep. Revision, not easily stopped, kept on. She dreamt of the words of the speech she had meticulously crafted. She dreamt of the gala that would follow. Important figures were judging her, eyes on her every move. She felt watched. Observed.

Someone touched her hand.

Hypatia slowly dragged herself from the dream gala.

A hand drew back from hers as she opened her eyes, and the hand's owner straightened up—he must have been leaning over to touch her. He must—

—HE!

She sat up quickly enough to make her head rush as the blood left her face.

"Morning, Aeych," the stranger said.

It was him. She looked up. Directly into his eyes. They were exactly as she had remembered them. They were searching and surveying her. His expression turned brooding, deepening the facial creases and ageing his appearance. *That isn't age*, she thought, *it's experience. Scars of adventure.*

Finally his look changed to one of confusion.

Why are those beautiful eyes confused?

"Plan on talking?" the stranger asked. "I don't mind you just staring, but usually 'Good morning' gets a response."

Oh no, she thought, *I've just been staring at him. No wonder he's confused.*

"Maybe I could prompt you?" he continued. "Good morning, Jet." He paused. "That's my name."

Oh goodness— Hypatia panicked, and hurried to fix her silence by blurting, "Good morning Hypatia!"

For a moment Jet's confusion reached a whole new level, then he broke out laughing.

Hypatia laughed too, half in nervousness and half in embarrassment.

"Not a morning person, I guess?" he asked.

"I'll have you know, mornings are not my strong point. Not before coffee, at least. Even worse, though, is being awakened by . . ." She paused; she didn't want to call him "a stranger." He wasn't a stranger, as he had been in her thoughts constantly for the last few nights.

"Jet."

"What?"

"My name is Jet."

"Right. Okay. Jet, then."

"Nice to meet you officially, Aeych."

"Hypatia. My name isn't Aeych."

"I know. But that name is too long to say in a hurry. Like, by the time you say, 'Watch out, Hypatia!' the roof has caved in. Instead, 'Aeych, look out!' and you're safe."

"The engineers and architects of the Library did not build a roof worthy of such concern." Hypatia knew she was still babbling, but was unable to control it.

"That's not what I meant. I mean, like" —he tried to make his point clearer by using exaggerated hand gestures— "pick any dangerous situation. One where you have to get out fast. You find you have to shout, 'Hypatia Theon of Iskendar, Great Librarian also known as The Catalogue!'" Jet paused, apparently having a sudden thought. "Oh well, I guess I could call you Cat."

"That's terrible."

"Aeych, then. Hi Aeych, I'm Jet."

"Good morning, Jet."

"Good morning."

There was silence as neither knew what to say next. Not to look foolish again, Hypatia was the first to speak this time. "Is now when you do your disappearing trick?" She pointed to a leather-bound volume belted to his waist.

"No, not yet. Aren't you surprised that I know who you are?"

"Not really. Everyone on Iskendar has heard about my appointment."

"What if I'm not from Iskendar?"

He didn't look like he was. Hypatia had not seen, read about, or heard of the style of dress he wore. She had definitely never seen another person vanish in front of her eyes before. "Where are you from, then?"

"Maybe someday I'll show you."

"Why so coy, secretive?"

"There's a lot you don't understand, Aeych." She liked hearing him say her name that way. "If I give you all the details at once, you'll go into shock. A mumbling mess, I would wager."

"I can handle a lot." She emphasized "a lot" exactly as he had said it, trying to make it clear to him that she could deal with that specific secret.

"I don't doubt that. But, trust me, it is a huge leap, like a monstrous ravine of logic you have to cross and, to some extent, put your faith in."

Faith was something new to Hypatia. Logic governed her world. However, undeterred—in fact, emboldened—she said, "Try me." She sounded more defiant than she had intended, partially because as she said it, she stood up.

He smiled and stepped toward her. Cocking an eyebrow, he stared into her eyes. "Not. Yet."

"When?"

"Two nights from now, I'll show you a little."

"I have a gala."

"I know. I've seen the news about your gala. I like your speech."

"You've been reading it."

"No. You were reciting it. Over and over again. In your sleep."

"How long were you watching me?" She wasn't disturbed that he had been watching her, only curious.

"Not so much watching as checking up on you as I read." He motioned to the stack of books Hypatia hadn't noticed on the table. "After the gala, meet me here."

"Jet, I—"

"Time for me to go." He pulled the book from his hip, unstrapping and dropping it open in one movement. He lowered his gaze to it and she immediately missed seeing his mesmerizing blue eyes. He spoke low, intentionally hiding the words from her.

All the noise of the previous night roared up again. Pages on pages turning. This time, despite the rising tide of an ocean of sound, she watched him. It started slowly. Jet's image was separated into a series of still pictures instead of flowing movement. The moments between his actions were being torn away, the gap widening as those images slowed, then stretched into a single line. Again the wave of noise climbed to a roar, suddenly broke, and he was gone. An echo of the roar ran the height of the Library, then washed away.

Even as shocked as she was at what she just witnessed, Hypatia sighed as she turned back to the table and saw a pile of books strewn about her own work.

"He didn't even put his books away."

CHAPTER SEVEN

Punctuated by outbursts of chatter, laughter, and general excitement, the audience for Hypatia's inaugural address filed into the auditorium in an orderly fashion. The first address of the Assistant to the Great Librarian was taking place in the largest outdoor forum in the Capital. The seating was a 180 degree-wide fan of stone benches descending to a small carpeted proscenium. The design made for clarity of sound no matter the position in the forum or the volume of attendees.

Speeches, especially large public affairs like Hypatia's inaugural address, were common on Iskendar. Seating was reserved for official attendants, so Hypatia knew that the mayor had yet to arrive in what might more aptly be called his private box—prime seating with all kinds of lavish comforts and cushions in place of the average stone bench.

Formal lecture etiquette was taught in school from a young age and practiced by everyone. Even without Hypatia raising a hand to signal for quiet, the audience of over one thousand were settling themselves naturally. With the energized excitement of the gathered throngs, Hypatia was impressed that it wasn't devolving into a rambling mess.

She felt comfortable as the centre of it all. This forum was her forum. She owned it. In any other private atmosphere, where the questions were equally as personal as professional, she could be uncomfortable. Sometimes she was speaking before her brain could form a proper response, the result lacking the intelligence, wit, and structure she showed on formal occasions. Hypatia was aware of the dichotomous nature of the introvert and expert parts of herself. Right now the expert, The Catalogue, was in control.

Sensing the audience was ready, she raised her hand.

Thousands of voices fell silent before her fingers reached their apex. The motion appeared to have sucked up all the noise with a single sweep. Dropping her arm, she opened her mouth to speak.

The voice of the mayor cut in before words could leave her mouth. "Welcome all!" He was behind her, and Hypatia jumped in surprise. "Thank you for coming!" His voice carried easily throughout the large space. The amphitheatre was designed to transport voices from the stage evenly and loudly to all parts of the forum, and Oren's rich, exuberant tone commanded the room.

"Our Iskendar is rich with history and passion. This history, this passion, is on the faces and in the hearts of every citizen." He was addressing the crowd but gesturing directly at Hypatia. "Your words are our words. Your thoughts are our thoughts. Your future is the future of everyone who shares that passion."

Hypatia had stepped back from the centre stage, slightly annoyed that he got the first word. Hiding her frustration, she feigned pride for the mayor's words. *Wrap it up*, she thought, anxious to start.

"Our future is paved with the words of our past. Forever has the Great Library and its caretakers lit the way. Today, we begin a new volume." He paused for effect. "A new *catalogue*." He paused again to allow the wave of excitement to pass through the crowd as he hit on the buzz word. "Please welcome the new Assistant to the Great Librarian!" He extended his arm toward Hypatia in a flourish.

Was his sole purpose for this introduction to make that pun? she wondered, and concluded that it likely was. Hypatia moved forward as he stepped down from the stage, already beginning to speak. She took up a position at centre stage for the opening, as had been her plan.

"Words are powerful. Alone they can be strong in their own isolated definitions. Words are made more powerful, impactful, when used to construct arguments and hypotheses. I argue here, today, that words are at their most influential in their absence." A murmur rippled through the crowd at the unexpected tack of her argument. "This will be a study of the redaction of Iskendar's history and what it portends for Iskendar's future." *A good opening*, she thought. *Not too forceful or laden with jargon.*

She settled into the speech from there. Over the course of the next hour there were calls of agreement and support from the assembled crowd. Kalli was there, in the front, nodding when Hypatia dove into the more complex nuances of how and why history had been shaped by the words that were left out. It seemed that everyone was on her side, and by the end she had them hanging on each word with excitement.

In complete contrast to her comfort on stage, Hypatia felt useless at the dinner gala that followed. In her first official appearance as the Assistant to the Great Librarian, she could not find the right words to say or hear the subtext she was normally skilled at lifting from others. She stumbled on facts she had known for years and made terrible puns. She knew people were whispering disappointments when they walked away.

A lightness in her chest that she struggled to suppress was distracting her. She knew it was Jet. He created an excitement like nothing that had infected her before, and it was breaking any focus she attempted to create.

"Hypatia," the mayor said, abruptly pulling her attention from picturing her hand moving through Jet's hair. "You are not yourself tonight."

"I, uh . . . know, sir." She dismissed the image of Jet with some difficulty. "The new position and the responsibilities are overwhelming. It's so much so fast, I think."

"Perhaps we have been rushing you. I'll have to speak to the Librarian and see if we can get you involved in a few projects that are up your alley. A new historical study on the founding of Iskendar could be timely during this period of change, don't you think?"

Hypatia perked up. Her graduating thesis and most of the papers she had written were about the landing of the *Arcadia* and the first settlers. Nearly ten thousand years were spent forming the planet before the Founders even touched ground. Since then, nearly another ten thousand years had passed. The literature on the subject was extensive. "Oh, that would be most . . ." She struggled to remain calm, as this was a dream project for her. "Appreciated."

Despite her conservative choice of words, the mayor could tell he'd struck a chord. He smiled and said, "Now go and impress them."

"Yes, Mayor; thank you."

"And please, Hypatia, don't call me mayor. My name is Oren."

"Yes, Oren; thank you."

The subject of Iskendar pushed thoughts of Jet from her mind for the rest of the night. The discussions she participated in after speaking with Oren would be the highlight of intellectual circles for months following the dinner. The Catalogue, as she was so often called, was on full display.

Energized by Oren's suggestion, she grounded herself in the stories of the how the first settlers, fresh from the landing of their ark, the *Arcadia*, shed the technology of the past and returned to agriculture. Understanding the universe through math and philosophy reigned.

Hypatia regaled dignitaries with details and insights on the slow pace of development on Iskendar. Basic electricity and a few other conveniences were allowed, as it made life easier and safer, but tools needed to study and make new discoveries required approval by committee. "For example, it took three hundred years for the committee to allow telescopes," she told a group of men who attempted to look as if this was all knowledge they already possessed.

Hypatia was in a particularly long conversation with the Professor of Evolution when she realized that the moment of Jet's return was drawing close. She'd been feigning interest in details she already knew, which made it easy for her mind to drift back to Jet.

"Most sentient life on Iskendar has its origins in the animals that stowed away on the *Arcadia*," he was saying. "Many creatures have developed traits that fit the environmental requirements unique to our planet."

Needing an out from the conversation, she interjected with, "The sprel fruit. Poisonous to rats, but it can be consumed by cockroaches." The professor looked puzzled. "A rat can, however, eat any number of cockroaches that dine on the fruit. So a rat *could* eat a sprel, but only a digested one. This is where the sprel gets its nickname, the Second-Hand Fruit."

The professor smiled at having learned something new and pulled a pen and paper from his pocket, muttering, "I must remember to mention this to . . ." He trailed off into his own thought and Hypatia slipped away from him and the nearly empty ballroom.

Grabbing a candle illuminating a poster advertising the events of the evening, Hypatia made her way out into the night. The forum was only a block from the Library; a few minutes later she stood in front of the doors to the ancient building.

The doors were locked. There was little crime on Iskendar, but the contents of the Great Library were too precious to leave unattended when everyone was at the gala, so the Library had been closed. Hypatia pulled out her key and slipped it into the lock. As the doors slowly swung open she could see flickering light on the high ceilings. She darted in, shut the doors behind her, locked them, and headed toward the light.

Rounding a large stack of books on the study of stars, she saw Jet sitting at a small desk, a candle before him illuminating a thick book he was staring at intently. The candlelight heightened Jet's furrowed brow and the roughness of his face. Hypatia admired it for several moments before Jet looked up at her.

He smiled, closed the book, and rose. Crossing the distance between them, he held out his hand without saying a word. She reached toward it and he grasped her hand with a strength and firmness that surprised her. Swinging the leather-bound book up from his side, he flicked aside the ties that bound the cover and flipped to a marked page, all with a single hand.

He looked up at her and smiled slyly. "Hold on."

CHAPTER EIGHT

He looked down at the book and words drifted from his mouth. They rode on his escaping breath.

Starting quietly at first, the sound of pages turning came drifting up from a distance and began to fill her ears. The noise rose shockingly fast. Hypatia instinctively brought her free hand up to block out the sound. The volume of it continued increasing, as if a thousand books, a million pages, were joining the cacophony. A Library full of pages beat past, darkening her world. The clamour of sound pressed down on her with a nearly unbearable weight. It reached a crescendo, then suddenly—

Silence.

All sounds ceased as if they had been swallowed.

The cool, dry air of the Library disappeared, replaced by nothing, as if the environment had died around her in a moment.

"Open your eyes." Jet sounded like he was talking through a thick fabric. She felt his lips on her ear.

The experience had left her nauseous. When she opened her eyes, her nausea was struck down by shock.

The sky was dark and starless. Only a single moon lit the landscape. An ocean was before her and it was filled with blackness a thousand miles wide. They stood upon the edge of a massive cliff. The ground, the cliffs, and the rocks below were made of glass. They reflected back the moonlight as the dark ocean crashed silently at its feet. A strong wind was blowing. Hypatia could see it tossing her dress about. Her hair had broken free of its bindings, and locks of her auburn hair fluttered with all the ribbons she had used to tie it back.

Complete silence filled her ears.

She could see the noise of the world, but something was stealing it away before it could exist.

Hypatia turned to look at Jet. He was holding her so close her nose grazed his cheek as she turned. His eyes were gigantic pools before her, full of excitement and hurt in the same moment. They held back all the words he was unable to say. Nervous at a suddenly intimate moment, Hypatia looked away again.

Jet slid his hand from her grasp to her back and pulled her body close but she kept her focus on the silent ocean. They stood together for a very long and contemplative embrace, staring at the silence of this foreign world. Hypatia struggled to come to terms with this reality.

In a burst of excitement she tore away from Jet and began running. She could feel him attempting to grab her but she had no intention of stopping now. Understanding was being consumed by some madness, incomprehension and a need to know. It was all so very new and Hypatia was driven to take in as much of it as she could.

As she ran soundlessly across the landscape, the sea crashing inaudibly beside her, Hypatia's mind tried to fill in the gaps where the sound of waves smashing on the shore and the roar of wind should be.

Turning on her toes as she ran, Hypatia started sliding across the surface. The ground was a hard glass far smoother than anything on Iskendar and providing no traction. Jet came into view as she spun and Hypatia saw the panic on his face. He was silently screaming and pointing past her. It occurred to her, at this point, that sliding was not something she knew how to stop doing. Even the spinning action was beyond her control. The landscape in front of her whirled back into her line of sight as Jet spun out of it, not because she wanted to see where she was going, but because it was no longer her choice.

A ghost of a scream escaped her lips as Hypatia realized what was coming.

What had been a sliver of a crack when she first glimpsed it was widening. *Not widening*, she thought. *I'm getting closer.*

As she slid toward the crack, it grew quickly to the width of a ditch. Moments later it was a crevasse, then a valley expanding into a gaping maw. Hypatia kept sliding, her panic increasing with her proximity.

Her body spun away from the approaching cliff, and impending doom, back toward Jet. She saw only the endless glass landscape before her.

Jet was gone.

She closed her eyes in fear as her body rotated back toward the cliff.

Strong arms grabbed her and, for a moment, they slid together. Then they slowed to a stop.

His arms were wrapped around her waist with his chest at her back. She could feel his breathing, hard and fast. She guessed hers felt the same to him.

"Open your eyes," he shouted in a whisper.

She did.

They were feet from the canyon. It was miles wide and covered in dark shimmering glass. The ocean, surging forward, drained into the canyon. The waves met the edge and cascaded into an unbelievable waterfall, the water disappearing out of sight far below. Billions of gallons of water were emptying into this scar cut into the planet.

It was massive. This was the only thing Hypatia had ever seen worthy of being called "epic." And it was as silent as the rest of the world.

She heard Jet's voice, a thousand miles away, shouting.

The approaching sounds of pages turning grew in Hypatia's ears. It seemed even louder this time as it replaced the infinite silence that surrounded them. The world disappeared and they landed on the floor of the Library, a few feet from the desk where she had seen Jet earlier.

Hypatia drew in a breath as if she had been starving for air then let it out, loudly. "What was that?"

"It takes some explaining," Jet said, wiping his brow.

"Try me, because right now it makes zero sense." Thoughts and beliefs Hypatia had always held began a battle inside her head with the new information thrust upon her senses moments before. The panic she'd felt when death neared fuelled her need for answers. "Everything I believed and this is . . . is what—"

"It was another world."

"Another world?"

"Yes."

"Okay, another world." She rose and stood thinking, trying to accept his answer, then leaned heavily on the small desk, searching for breath she seemed unable to completely take in. "Give me the how. How is that possible?"

"Here is what I think," he said, also getting to his feet and stuffing the leather book back into its pouch. "The universe is tied together on an endless string. Your world, that world, and all the others are the loops and knots and weft. I travel that string on the minds of creative genius. The words of so many of humanity's writers and poets and musicians are torn from the tapestry the string makes. If you can feel it, the right passage of a story, a verse in a song or poem, you can read it aloud and be taken to another world." He paused for what Hypatia thought could only be dramatic effect before finishing with, "The words move us."

"Us? You aren't the only one?"

"We call ourselves gatewrights. We build gates like a shipwright builds ships, using words."

"Or like a playwright builds a play, I suppose." This was all a little much for Hypatia, but her logic needed to find reason here.

Jet processed what Hypatia had said as if it was some revelation he had never considered. A smile crept onto the corners of his mouth. He laughed, the noise echoing through the vacant Library. She was comforted by his voice bouncing off objects in the Library.

"Yeah." He was still laughing. "I guess that is exactly what it is. You have a way with words, Aeych."

"That world," she said, needing to voice what she felt. "It was beautiful and yet I felt so sad." Jet appeared unsurprised. He stayed silent, sensing her excitement. "Sometimes no matter how much you wish something wouldn't happen, it does. It feels like simply thinking about it brings it into being,"

Jet reacted by stepping back from her, as if attempting to bring her into focus. "How can you tell that from just seeing it?"

"I saw it there and I see it in you. You shared your home and, I think, your history." Looking at him, she'd seen the sadness of losing everything in his eyes when they stood on the cliff. She yearned to take away his pain with every fibre of her being. She barely knew Jet, but wanted everything from him, for him.

"I see them still, Aeych. Every time I go back there." She saw his pain as he spoke. "My friends playing, my mother offering lunch, my dog running toward me." He looked away from her. "I push it out of my mind, but a guilt I don't deserve always creeps back in." Hypatia moved to close the distance between them and he put up his hand to stop her. "Years. It's been years since it happened and it comes back to me like it was only yesterday."

"You can play it over a million times," she said, trying to comfort him with her understanding, "how you could have changed it."

"That isn't right. It was determined. I am guilty but my home was lost before I could stop it." He pulled the book from its pouch so quickly, Hypatia didn't notice until he was already opening it. "This was a stupid idea. I fell for your—" He stopped there and looked down at the book. "I'll be back. Two days from now, after lunch or brunch or whatever you have here. Meet me." He spoke something more and Hypatia was certain again that it wasn't in a language she knew. The actual words he used eluded her.

The pages, the wind, and the flashes came without any warning. In an instant, Jet was gone.

As the air settled, Hypatia could feel someone watching her.

"Your speech was impressive," Kalli said, "but this would steal the thunder of your message. Literally."

Feeling she needed to explain herself, Hypatia said hurriedly, "That was Jet. He does this travelling . . ." She was at a loss; what explanation could she provide?

"I heard," Kalli said. "He's a gatewright. Or that's what they call themselves."

Thinking Kalli shared in her excitement, Hypatia cut in with, "It's so fascinating! And he—"

"Be careful, Hypatia." Kalli's authoritative tone stopped her words and shredded her excitement. "This requires counsel. Oversight from a committee."

Hypatia didn't like the idea of her journey coming under the scrutiny of an elected panel. The formality would drain all the romance out of it. She couldn't imagine Jet sitting through an inquisition. He'd wave off the high-level diplomats with a sweep of his hand and a "Don't bother yourself with the details." She believed she knew Jet deeply already. The Catalogue part of her whispered to be careful at that thought.

"I don't say this from a position of superiority. I am not acting as the Librarian riding on her power," Kalli said. "The whole affair is dangerous, girl."

"Oh, I know. I saw it." Being called "girl" made her feel smaller.

"I suspect the danger you know is nothing to which I refer. If it were, you would hide beneath one of these desks and struggle for sanity you can no longer grasp." Kalli's shadow appeared to grow longer as she continued. "There are horrors that Iskendar is protecting you from. It protects us all. When they wright—even with the stranger just being here—you weaken the walls."

"Weaken the walls?" Hypatia had been clutching her arms to her chest. Noticing this, she tried to relax them.

"The Founders knew. They also warned us that knowing would bring risk. They called the impending apocalypse a chaos."

Hypatia felt defiant. She was intelligent and could make informed decisions. "Nothing has harmed this world in all of its ten thousand-plus years. What could be so fearsome to know?"

"No visitor has ever been to our world in all recorded history, either. Search your Catalogue. You have no mention of wrights in the past."

She knew immediately there was nothing on the subject.

"When you have been Great Librarian for some time, long after I am gone, you will find out why." Kalli pulled a periodical from a nearby shelf. "Perhaps sooner. You are the youngest assistant in history. Another worldly stranger. All these firsts. Could it be an omen?"

Hypatia was shocked at her reference to an omen. "We are a people of logic. Omens are not worth broken stones."

"When logic can explain how he wrights, I'll feel better about omens."

Hypatia was trying to formulate a possible answer but the logic kept slipping away from her. There were too many holes in what was known as possible for her to explain wrighting. It was as if she was being teased with the answer, and then it slipped under murky waters.

"Focus on your study. Focus on your family. Be what the people of Iskendar believe you to be," said Kalli.

Knowing her place, Hypatia dutifully answered, "Yes, of course, my librarian."

Hypatia was thinking about what dangerous things Kalli might already know as she disappeared into the darkness a few floors below.

CHAPTER NINE

For her fourth birthday, Hypatia had received her first book without pictures.

Until then nothing had indicated her future ability—almost everything she'd learned had been delivered through speech and absorbed through listening. When Hypatia learned to read, the ability flipped a switch in her mind. She took to books like a leaf to the wind. Her reading levels skipped from preschool to middle grades in less than a complete changing of the seasons as she sat flipping through pages, eyes wide, mouth flat in concentration.

With reading came her remarkable speaking skills. The more Hypatia read, the more she had to say. She regurgitated myths, histories, legends, and fairy tales on command and whenever she felt like it. Her recollection was flawless, not only of facts, but precise ancillary details—metaphors, similes, references to other stories, she absorbed it all.

In the retelling of any story, she could energize the imagery. Other children, and increasingly more adults, would ask to hear her animated accounts of historical fables.

When she got her first chapter book, Hypatia was ecstatic. The words were no longer trapped by the limited scribbles of the children's book illustrator.

Her first book was an ancient tale predating even the Founders: *Alice and the Magic Mirror*, in which a schoolgirl chased a rodent down a hole and was beset by game pieces, poetry, and extravagant riddles. Hypatia was Alice and she was going to Wonderland to meet a knight or a giant moth. Other books would come and go from her favourites list, but there was always something different about *Alice*. It transported her away.

One night Hypatia was upset when she read a different tale, about an indescribable monster from a murky lake tormenting a poor villager. She was upset not because the story was too scary, but because the writer could not describe the monster. She sought the solace of *Alice's* words instead. The author, long forgotten, skillfully imagined a nightmare beast

with eyes of flames,
came whiffling through
the tugly wood
and burbled as it came.

Hypatia stood in a dark forest. The trees bent and grew unnaturally. They reached out in all directions. As they'd grown, the limbs pushed past each other, often growing over and then back on themselves. Knots formed countless times on many trees with no clear rhyme or reason. Bare limbs devoid of foliage managed to look healthy and felt alive to Hypatia despite all appearances. The trees were breathing, rapid and shallow.

In her hand Hypatia held a dagger. It glowed with veins of green pulsing light that criss-crossed over its surface. The ambient light of the dagger illuminated only the nearest of the trees, unable to penetrate the darkness that bound those beyond. The shadows cast by the pulsing green glow danced as she twisted the weapon, trying to see deeper into the woods.

A cracking of branches and scratching of metal shuddered through the trees, and they groaned. A gurgling chitter echoed rhythmically from the forest. The cracking and scratching noises made her jump as they surged around her.

"Beware."

A cascade of metal scraping and crashing was capped by a tremor that rattled in Hypatia's teeth. A blast of wind shot into the grove and grasped at the light of the dagger, trying to smother it. It dimmed only briefly.

The forest darkened around her and Hypatia could see the eyes of a monster. Its pupils were alight with flame. Dark red and orange fire burned from the wrath of a million years into her mind. A pulse of pain burrowed inside her head, but her fear held back a response. She wanted to scream. Tears forced their way into her eyes and made it even harder to see.

The beast smashed forward, dragging its snakelike body with such strength and swiftness that the trees lay down before it, as if to honour it. Hypatia let out a squeal and instinctively raised the dagger in front of her with both hands.

A claw swung out from the monster and dashed the glowing blade from her grip. She felt the claw slice through the skin of her arm as if it were cheap paper. The weapon skidded along in the dirt and everything went dark.

Except the flames.

The eyes grew larger and she could feel the heat of the fire glowing within them. The teeth of the monster, shards of metal, rusted, jagged, and innumerable, glinted dully in the light of the fire.

The monster opened its maw. The stench and heat of its breath, like a polluted sauna, suffocated her. As the massive jaws reached their apex, the monster lunged forward. Hypatia tried to jump backward to avoid the metal jaws.

"Hypatia!"

Her mother was shaking her. Her legs slammed into a play kitchen in her bedroom as she fell to the floor.

Tears flowed from her eyes as a whimper escaped her throat. Her mother grabbed her, softly stroked her hair, and whispered, trying to calm her down. Hypatia relaxed, then felt a warm liquid running down her arm. She looked down. Her floor, her dress, and her mother were covered in blood.

She lifted her hand and a ragged flap of skin hung from the back of it.

The world dimmed around her.

Hypatia was in her adult room. Her mother was gone but the blood was real.

CHAPTER TEN

Hypatia didn't spring awake from her vivid nightmare. *Was that a dream or a memory?* she wondered, staring at the ceiling.

She was still holding her hand above her. A small drop of blood grew from the bottom of her clenched fist. It hesitated, threatening to fall.

"It was real."

The drop fell. It seemed to hang in the air, taking an eon to move.

"It was real." She realized distantly that she was speaking to herself.

The droplet splattered onto her lips and spilled down the corner of her mouth to trickle down her jaw and behind her head.

She felt like she was at the bottom of a well, looking up, but lacking the energy or desire to get out. Her oxygen was running out, yet she didn't feel the need to struggle.

"I should panic."

Drip.

This drop barely missed her open mouth, splattering on her chin before creeping down her neck.

Feeling the blood dribble down, Hypatia pictured her face covered in tiny red rivers. She was reminded of the next gift her mother had gotten her. A globe. The books were taken away in short order after that night. Not locked away, but inconvenient for her to get at. The globe took centre stage in her room instead.

Hypatia would drag friends and family to her room to see the globe. It stood on a pedestal as high as her head when she received it. She would point and name as many of the places she could, then beam with pride every time an adult remarked, *"Wow,"* and *"Isn't she so bright?"*

As Hypatia grew, the globe would be the homes of the great

philosophers or the guide to the schools of thought on Iskendar: a map of the libraries, discoveries, and political centres. It became the store for her knowledge. If she needed to recall something, she could remember it by finding its place on the globe. Slowly the globe, and all the knowledge she kept within it, took up residence in her mind.

Drip.

The Catalogue was born of her fear of fiction. The reality of what the stories had become threatened her sanity and her life. In the days following the dream, her mother replaced the stories and fairy tales with works of history, math, and geography. Hypatia loved to learn, imagining how the people and places of Iskendar filled the globe with life.

Drip.

Turning her head, Hypatia could see the stars clearly in the night sky. She sat up for a better look. *If anyone looked in at this moment,* she thought, *they would run screaming.* Her face, reflected in the window, was a crimson mask.

She giggled at the idea. Then she openly laughed at the thought of a blood-soaked woman in the dark, laughing insanely at her own appearance.

Someone was screaming.

Hypatia sat bolt upright in the hot morning sun. Her mother was staring at her. Seeing her covered in dried blood, Aurelia screamed again.

"Mom! Mom! Stop it!" Hypatia threw her hands up to cover her ears.

Her mother drew in a breath and threw her own hand to her mouth.

Hypatia's head hurt and the dried blood made her skin itchy. When her mother stopped screaming Hypatia awkwardly grabbed her arm with one hand and scratched her cheek with the other. Blood flaked off onto the sheets. The flakes blended into the stains that covered the bed. *No wonder she was screaming.*

"What happened?" Aurelia was still gasping for air as she rushed to the bed and embraced her daughter.

Stunned momentarily, Hypatia couldn't remember where the blood had come from. "I . . ."

"I was so scared," her mother said.

"There was a monster." She was beginning to remember. "In the trees. When I was a girl."

Aurelia grabbed her shoulders and held her at arm's length. "Don't say that. Why would you say that?"

"Because—" her mother was staring into her eyes with a fierceness she couldn't recall seeing before "—it's what I saw."

"You promised. We promised." Her mother's voice broke and Hypatia realized she was shaking. Hypatia could hear it in her voice and feel it in her grip. She winced as her mother's fingers clamped down on her shoulders.

Her mother pulled her in close and started stroking her hair. "It can't be.

47

No, it's over. Always over." She sounded more like she was assuring herself than comforting Hypatia. Her mother gripped her with full force for a moment. Then, sniffing loudly, she released Hypatia's shoulders and sprang to her feet. She straightened her own dress, now stained with smears of dried blood. "Oh my." Her tone had become matronly. "You are a mess, Hypatia. Now get yourself cleaned up at once." Turning to leave, she paused and regarded her own defiled clothing before saying, "When you are finished, bring those clothes and sheets and—" she waved her arms without turning back "—anything else that needs to be cleaned."

Before Hypatia could add anything or reply to her mother, Aurelia had stepped out and closed the door to her room.

Brunch was marred with awkward silence. They ate under a broad olive tree in the garden. It shaded the stone patio and the dark-stained wooden table.

Hypatia scratched softly at the bandages her mother had applied to her torn arm as she studied the tree.

The silence was broken when Hypatia's father swallowed a bite of egg and started coughing. Grabbing his juice to wash down the offending piece of egg, he knocked a pitcher from the table between himself and Hypatia. It shattered as it struck the ground. "I'll—" cough "—get—" cough.

"You stop," said Hypatia. "You can't even string two words together. Have a drink." She slid her cup over to him and stood. "I'll clean this."

Her mother clapped her father on the back unhelpfully. He coughed again. "Thank you. I'm a little out of sorts this morning."

"We all are," her mother added with a look on her face that said there was a giant weed in the garden no one wanted to talk about.

Hypatia cleaned up the pieces of broken pitcher and walked a few feet to the garbage. With her back to the table she asked, "I'd like you to tell me what happened. I need to know."

"Oh, well, I guess I was distracted with the egg and I bit off a bit more than I could chew."

"When I was young," Hypatia said without turning. "This dream." Each phrase came out calculated. "This dream or this memory. It was a memory, I'm sure. Something so tangible I could smell it. I could taste it. In my room when I was young. I can taste the metal in my mouth from it."

"That could have been your brain picking up the cues from the real world," her mother suggested. "You were pretty bloody, especially about the face." She sounded like she was holding back tears.

"Before that. In the woods." Hypatia was speaking slowly, picturing the events as they'd happened, "I felt the breath of the monster on me. I could smell burning coal and wet rot. Never have I been so afraid, but I must have been. I must because I remember it."

"I think I would recall if this happened," said her father. "I would think you would remember too."

She returned to the table wiping the residue from the broken pitcher off her hands. "You and Mom," she said without malice, "worked so hard to make me forget it. Gave me textbooks on math and philosophy." She paused. "And my globe. You were pushing me toward academics."

"Fiction really isn't for the politically minded, Aeych," her mother said.

"That isn't it. I see the look in your eyes." She stared at her mother, taking her hands across the table. "Fear."

Her mother looked down and shifted in her seat.

"Hypatia," Quint started.

"No, Quint. It's alright." Aurelia reached over to grip his arm to stop him from continuing. "If we hide it any longer it won't benefit anyone. We can't pretend."

"Thank you, Mom."

Her mother snapped at her, "Now don't you go thinking I want to tell you, because I don't. If I could take this to my grave, I would in a heartbeat." She stopped talking to look at her husband, who nodded as if in approval.

"When you were little you had these dreams. They were recurring, for months on end. Not just the monster of *Alice*, but creatures and people from all kinds of stories. They would visit you at night."

"Then," her father started, but Aurelia again cut him off.

"Let me tell it, Quint. I need to get this off my chest. My way."

He coughed quietly and took a drink, looking uncomfortable.

"The things started to visit you in the daytime, too. We never saw them."

"The Capsias' boy died," Quint added abruptly.

"That's what his parents said." Aurelia was quick to cut him off again, shooting him a look. "But that boy had such an imagination. He told me once he heard a god speaking to him."

"Is this relevant, Mother?"

"In a way." The words spilled from her. "He loved fiction as much as you. He was as bright as you."

"Ahem," Quint interjected, trying to lighten the mood.

"A father's pride," Aurelia said, acknowledging Quint and using the break to slow herself down. "He was a very smart boy, but not as bright as our beloved daughter. We only heard snippets of what happened to him. Rumours of a voice he heard were only rumours to us. The papers said it was tragic and unexpected and that was all."

"But—" Quint tried to add.

"But I spoke to his mother," Aurelia continued, not giving him a chance to say more, "and at first I thought she was attempting to find reason or fault for his death. She told me he could describe places he'd never seen in vivid detail. Beyond a normal child's simple imagination or fantasy. He could identify people and places with full names, descriptions, events, and histories. He reminded me so much of you and your dreams. The problem really started, though, with a place he called—" She turned to Quint. "Oh, what was it again?"

"Eftal."

She dropped right back into the story. "Eftal was progress. Electric lights, electric sounds, and electric machines. Machines that did the work of the everyday, too—cooking, cleaning, and transportation. People wore technology and used it as a part of their bodies. They lived and breathed the sort of progress that Iskendar has shunned. He had friends there and could tell stories about the things they did. There was always extremely fine detail to it all. The weird part, the convincing part, was his consistency. The consistency made it impossible to ignore. He would correct the names when his mother tried to repeat the stories, adding more information about the day to day changes they went through, weaving an ever larger picture of a world. A world that only existed in his head."

"How could this be a bad thing?" Hypatia was confused. Eftal sounded much nicer than her own wonderland.

"The people, the fictional people, in the imaginary world changed. They were afraid. He was worried for their safety. I saw the young boy around this time and I swear he was mumbling something about chaos and destruction and he looked strained. A child of six looked like he was carrying the weight of the world on his heart." Tears formed at the edges of her eyes and she let out a sad sigh. "She said she should have taken it as a warning sign about his safety." She was struggling to get the words out. "But how could an imaginary world hurt her real son? What if it happened to you?"

Quint reached out and caressed her fingers. "Your mother and I had the same feelings when you had your nightmares. Recalling everything that happened to him made us feel helpless in the face of what was happening to you."

"How did he die?" The pain in her mother's voice tugged at Hypatia's heart, but she needed to know the answer to this question.

Quint spoke, seeing that Aurelia didn't want to say it. "He began digging one day. Just out in the yard. He tore at the ground. His mother tried to get him to stop and he was screaming as she pulled at him. The exhaustion or fear or something else took him. He started vomiting blood and sores opened up. Maybe they were caused by the frantic digging." He shrugged.

"He was bleeding out. None of that made it into the papers but one of the nurses or attendants leaked out the details of what they'd seen."

Hypatia's mother got up from the table, putting her hand to her face, and quickly walked to the patio doors.

Quint waited until she had made it into the house and cleared his throat. "His mother found the boy in a hole he had dug by hand. Two or three feet deep. They found him in the arms of his mother. She was covered in his blood." He paused and coughed but did not drink anything to chase it away. "The child had lacerations up his arms—nowhere else—and his hair was falling out. Not ripped out, just falling off of him."

Her father stopped talking. They sat in silence for a while, quietly finishing their meal. Quint tried to fill the silence by talking about the garden work they had been doing that previous week. Both Hypatia and her father were trying to bury the images and darkness the conversation had uncovered.

CHAPTER ELEVEN

Jet left her a note in the Library that night. The next day would be Jet's first planned visit to the city outside the Library and he hoped she would show him around.

Hypatia was eager to see him again. She felt safe in his strong presence. A part of her wanted her to be afraid too, but she pushed it down. Her anticipation of the visit drove all thoughts of the forest and the monster from her mind, and she slept easy the next day.

"The people are talking about us already," Jet said as they exited the Library that night. "I see them whisper when we pass, throwing glances our way."

Hypatia had noticed it too. "At least they are trying to be discreet about it." A pair of stately older men approaching them on the main road veered into a bookshop and watched the young couple through the window, mouths working in obvious discussion. "It's alright. That's what the people of this world do. Talk, talk, and talk. Gossip and rumour are minor, common varieties of talk."

"Gossip, eh?" Jet said with a sly smile.

"You are with the most influential, eligible woman on Iskendar." She wasn't boasting. To prove her point, she lifted a newspaper with a headline about The Catalogue from a local stand and handed it to him. "And look at the fashion around here. Is there anything like" —she gestured at his clothing— "those pants, your leather belt, and that dusty book you wear? You stick out."

"That's part of my appeal. My charm."

"Country bumpkin is your charm?"

"Exotic adventurer," he retorted proudly.

"Adventuring is not something we do on Iskendar—at the very least, not in the Capital."

"The idea of travelling somewhere new, taking barely what you need to survive and hoping that you have the wits to survive—" he gestured grandly "—that's romantic."

"In books it might be. In reality there is nowhere on this world we have not documented, studied, reviewed, and—"

" Catalogued."

"Ha. Ha. Ha," she said sarcastically.

"Why not go to space, then?" he said, glancing upward. "Reach for the endless galaxy. These people must be curious about what could be out there. You want to find where your people came from. You love history. Can you just imagine what history is out there?"

Hypatia wondered if he was intentionally trying to draw more attention to them. More gossip. "The Founders forbade it."

"Star travel?"

"Not specifically. Technology for star travel. Progress for progress. Iskendar offers everything we need."

"Except . . ."

"Except?" She cocked her head, puzzled.

"The unknown. No curiosity. No desire to seek out the mysteries of the universe and answer them. Without curiosity the heart, the mind, and the soul wither, contract, and, sooner or later, die."

"If that time comes, then, for survival, we will need to move forward with progress. But it will be at our own peril." She was watching the bookshop window, where the two men were still pretending to browse. "Our Founders spoke of danger. They set the boundaries to keep the endless horrors at bay."

"All worlds have legends."

She was angry that he dismissed it so easily. "It is not a legend. It is a rule—the only sacred commandment of Iskendar. Progress in science. Progress in technology. Progress for the sake of progress will bring—"

"Chaos," he said in unison with her.

She frowned and looked directly into his eyes. "How did you know?"

"I know chaos." His tone had become serious. "I fled from it. Saved others from it."

She switched from angry to excited. "The Founders were right?"

"No."

"No? Clearly you know of the chaos the Founders were protecting us from. How is this not the warning come to life?"

"Yes, it is." He wouldn't look at her.

"Yes? No? Which is it, Jet?"

"Progress. It isn't the progress that matters, Aeych. I can see why they might have thought that, but chaos is there no matter what you do or believe—or don't believe, I guess."

"So, progress?"

"Forbidding technological progress might slow it, delay an inevitable arrival for centuries. But the chaos is already here. You can find it. It's science and it's also art. It's philosophy and, worst of all, it's love." They were walking now. He was tense and she could tell he needed to be moving.

"And you adventure to save us from chaos."

"I do. I run from it, too."

She huffed. "Jet, you are terrible with clear answers. If we were to make a cake, it would be sweet and savoury and look like a pile of dirt."

"It's better for you that I am."

"I suppose you will warn me that you've said too much already."

"It's possible. You do that to me, make me say too much."

She took his hand. His face brightened and he smirked. "Oh, they are going to be talking about this." With his free hand, Jet motioned to their hands.

She pulled him to a stop. "No they won't." She pulled him into a hard kiss, not giving him a chance to think about it. He kissed back.

People stopped in the street to watch as the two most interesting people on the whole planet passionately kissed in the heart of the Capital. They remained locked in their kiss until they were forced up for air.

CHAPTER TWELVE

Gossip tore through the Capital like a deluge from a broken dam. It was, after all, a city populated by those who spent their lives sharing information. Talk was the most valuable currency, and the rate of trade was excellent when it came to the Assistant to the Great Librarian.

Being referred to as The Event, or more dramatically as The Stranger, the story of the two new lovers was shared in every neighbourhood of the Capital like waters flowing down the aqueducts. Since The Event was a single moment for Hypatia and Jet, the more suitable name referring to their relationship was The Catalogue and Her Vanishing Stranger.

Hypatia overheard this in an exchange between two dignitaries unaware of her eavesdropping. She was giddy at the thought of her and Jet being something worthy of gossip. *Perhaps they will make great stories of us and our blossoming romance*, she imagined.

Jet had come to Iskendar three times since their first meeting. On the last trip they had gone to the open community market held in the Capital, and he was amazed by the varieties of food on display. Jet was particularly interested in the fresh fish and fruits. He remarked over and over about the complex smells and the vibrant colours as he dragged her from one stall to the next.

Hypatia knew she was falling for him. Telling herself it was stupid, childish, and against every academic thought she held did nothing to soften her feelings. He was a part of her, a part that she'd never known she was missing. When Hypatia found herself distracted from study or work, she was off somewhere unexplainable and he was holding her back from the precipice of danger.

It was ridiculous, she thought, but she pictured Jet both encouraging and taming some wildness Hypatia had never been in touch with before.

Her imagination ran as wild as her spirit wanted to.

They were running through a forest, pursued by ferocious beasts baring sharp claws and sharper teeth. The creatures were gaining on them. She pumped her legs as fast as they could carry her. At her side, Jet was running both harder and faster, yet somehow completely in time with her own pace. When she stumbled he swept her up in his strong arms and threw her over his shoulder. His musky sweat and hot breath warmed her as he ran, putting distance between them and the monsters. Hypatia stared down at the snarling beasts with their sharp teeth and hungry eyes.

In another dream, she imagined the two of them back on the cliffs of the glass world, entwined in a deep embrace reminiscent of *The Verdant Thorn's* lurid cover. Silently the air streams were pulling at their clothes, threatening to bare their flesh. She could feel the heat and smell the adventure wafting from his cologne as he leaned in for the hero's kiss.

"Aeych."

She pulled him closer.

"Aeych, the Founders lived in squalor . . ."

Hypatia's mother had walked in. Slowly Hypatia pulled herself out of that amazing daydream.

"For months," Aurelia continued, "when the Founders left the *Arcadia*, they lived in squalor." She was bent over, picking up scattered books from the floor. "But even they wouldn't have put up with this mess."

Hypatia snapped into the present to retort, "I don't think the Founders were concerned with too many books, papers, or copies of old speeches, Mother."

"I'm saying there is no way you can be using all these books at the same time. You have—what?" She made a show of counting the resources scattered about Hypatia's room. "A thousand volumes here?" Hypatia's mother had always been prone to exaggeration.

"I could explain why I need each of these for my work, but as soon as I start talking about—" she picked up one volume and read the title "—*The Philosophies of the Arcadians*, your eyes start to glaze over."

"Oh, please don't. I have heard enough about how the Arcadians believed this or the Founders banned that to fill my own library. Really, Hypatia, what can we hope to learn from people who lived ten thousand years ago that hasn't already been studied, re-studied, pre-studied, under-studied, and studied again?"

"Well, first of all, Mother, one of those wasn't an actual word. And if you'd like to know the truth, I can tell how this comes together. Or maybe not how, but . . ." She started speaking as if to herself and Aurelia at the same time. "There are clues I keep finding. Like threads that speak to each other. And Jet—"

"Jet?" Aurelia let out a long, disapproving sigh, the kind of sigh that is only ever issued by mothers. "I think you spending time with this stranger" —Hypatia winced at the way her mother said the word stranger— "is a bad idea. He is using technology—" Hypatia was about to cut her off, but her mother continued, speaking louder as she sensed the impending argument "—technology that your Arcadian Founders would be against in all manner of ways."

"It isn't technology."

"If it isn't, then it makes no sense. If you can't explain it, and you can explain everything, then it must be some kind of magic."

"But it isn't magic, or even chaos. There are threads."

"Enough with magic, chaos, and threads. You are smart. Possibly the smartest person on Iskendar. Possibly the smartest person in the history of this world. But you are also quite young, Hypatia. I have to protect you from being manipulated and deceived. You could read every book ever written and it would not replace life experience. Trust your mother."

Hypatia wanted to argue, but thought better of it. "I trust you, Mom."

"Good. I know you don't, but thank you for pretending." She smiled warmly. "Now pick up this mess." Aurelia placed the books she had picked up on a flimsy tower of research papers.

Hypatia snatched a book from the top as the stack tipped and tumbled over onto the floor. Papers and books scattered along the stone tiles, several slipping under her bed and desk. A few, she discovered later, found their way under her closet door, as well.

Hypatia looked at the book she had saved. It was a poetry anthology and The Catalogue recalled a passage before she even read the title:

O love they die in yon rich sky
They faint on hill or field or river

Another snippet of a play written a hundred years later floated into her thoughts:

Oh that the desert were my dwelling place,
With only one fair spirit for my minister.

Her mind began working without conscious direction. It wasn't just the passage that was familiar, Hypatia realized, it was the repetition. Over a thousand years writers, poets, and other artists would hit on these same points. The Catalogue felt words flex somewhere deep in her mental globe. They weren't simply universal truths about love or death, but words that spoke of visceral places; a real world that you could reach out and touch.

A passage from a playwright written half a century before flew out from the globe and surfaced in her consciousness of its own accord.

> *But now the Northwind came more fierce,*
> *There came a Tempest strong!*
> *And Southward still for days and weeks*
> *Like Chaff we drove along.*

Hypatia could see the connections because The Catalogue was making the ideas come together without her involvement. The globe was spinning and throwing ideas off as it spun.

Her mind pulled out another quote. The source eluded her on this one—a rare but occasional occurrence—but it still fit the mold she was building.

> *The universe is a yawning chasm,*
> *filled with emptiness and the puerile meanderings of sentience.*
> *That good ship and true was a bone to be chewed*
> *When the gales of November came early*

Hypatia could see that while the landscape painted itself, the keys to gain access to it remained foreign.

Something hummed and growled within her.

When she tried to focus on the gate, everything slipped away. The connections she had been seeing blurred and no longer appeared logical. The rope she had been drawing in so quickly slid from her hands and was gone.

The thread broke and Hypatia snapped back to the book in her hand. She set it down on the desk and let out a breath. Wiping sweat from her brow, Hypatia noticed she could still hear her mother walking away from the room. *All that happened in a moment*, she thought, and then dismissed it, thinking her mother must have come back for something.

Knowing she would be unable to focus on her work, Hypatia took to collecting the papers and books strewn about the room. The more she worked on the cleanup, the more distant and imagined the thread became.

She decided she needed to take a break. Leaving with the better part of the mess contained, Hypatia set out to the heart of the Capital, seeking a change of scenery.

A short walk later she was sitting in the golden afternoon sun in a lush public garden, watching the bees buzzing from flower to flower with direction and purpose. For years of her life, she thought, nothing had changed. Hypatia began to wonder if anything on Iskendar would ever excite her again. She pictured the fertile season, followed by the clear warm seasons. Then came the dying season that circled back to fertile. Iskendar was always going through the motions and so would she. She would pave the road ahead year after year, making it easier for future generations as the Great Librarian.

She watched a bee drift lazily by and lost herself in thoughts of its dedication to the cycle of seasons and life. Hypatia had succeeded where no one else had in gaining such renown so quickly. Having achieved her life's goal younger than anybody else, she wondered: why was she searching for more?

The universe must hold so many wonderful and thrilling things for one to experience. Am I going to just march through life in my role of library assistant?

"There has to be more," she said to an oblivious rabbit nibbling on the lawn. It stopped briefly to twitch its ears and peer her way, as if it were listening—not to her specifically, but listening nonetheless. "Look at you," she went on. "You seem happy to just sit there and eat. No worries to speak of. You live in this moment with no expectations of what you should do with your time, no plan for what you need to become. You're free to do what animals will with no one to let down."

The bunny took off at top speed as heavy footsteps thudded closer. Hypatia could tell it was Jet without even looking.

"Why do you do it?" she asked. "How do you wright? How do you live with that life?"

She thought he would have to stew on the answer, as he did for so many things, but he responded as if they had been deep in conversation already. "I decided that the constant peril I've known was not what I wanted. That something had to be done." He sat down beside her. "I could tell that the universe was pulling apart at the seams, with all the darkness I have seen, and it wasn't going to change itself. You can't just stick bandages on an infection and expect it to heal. You have to treat the problem to get rid of it."

Jet was looking out into the horizon and the story of his years swept across his face in deep, shadowed lines. "Now I'm doing this for us, Aeych."

She didn't know what to say to this, but she felt her heart rate increase at the word "us."

Jet continued. "I have gatewrighted more times than I can even remember and I never cared about the outcome for myself. With you, I have something to look forward to. Someone to fight for." Jet's boldness in comparison to Gaius made her blush. "It makes these decisions to leave you, when I do, so much harder. I find myself questioning every call I make. Ideas I would have never second-guessed before now sit on my shoulders with the weight of a thousand worlds."

A silence followed. In that silence she thought she could feel the weight he was carrying.

"Sometimes, Aeych, I'm very much making this all up on the fly. In all this time, I'm battling something I don't quite understand. I just know that it can't go on like this or it will tear away at the universe. Our universe. I want you by my side, but right now by my side is the most dangerous place to be."

"Jet, I don't think I like what you are implying." She couldn't explain why, exactly, but she was angry and excited at that same time. "If you think I am just going to sit here and mind my manners while you flit off into a war against the universe, you need to shake your head. I know that is how you have always done it, but that was before me." Hypatia was surprised at her own boldness, but continued. "I will not hang around Iskendar, waiting to hear if you are okay. You can't say *us* and think I will play a bystander when I can be out there helping to fight the problem. More importantly, I'm not about to send you off on a suicide mission by yourself. I am with you whether you want me there or not, and that's my decision to make, not yours," she said with confidence but no suggestion of blame.

He nodded. After a few moments of silence, he stood. Having gotten what he wanted and feeling no need to add to the conversation, he departed without anymore words. Hypatia was disappointed that it had come and gone so quickly, but made no effort to chase after him. She stared off into the distance where the rabbit had disappeared.

The afternoon had become night before she knew it and Hypatia, still on the garden bench, stared up at the night sky, imagining where Jet might be.

"The stars make us look so small," Gaius said as he took a seat where Jet had been moments before. *No, not moments*, she thought, wondering how long she'd been sitting there. Had it been hours?

Instinctively she reached out to accept the hot cup of coffee she knew Gaius would have and, without dropping his own gaze from the sky, he handed the drink to her.

"All the speeches, town halls, and great proclamations—" He mockingly imitated the mayor: "This is the most important day in the history of Iskendar!" Dropping the sarcasm, he continued. "—and we think we are giants, our every step creating an impression in the ground that will last an eternity." He paused and studied the expanse above him, then sighed in reverence. "But Iskendar and all of its important history are a blink in the passage of time to the universe. Humanity, before and after, has forgotten and will forget every moment. Then, when the universe disappears with a tiny cry, it will only be a single note in a song of the infinite."

"That's really sad to try to imagine," Hypatia said before taking a sip and turning to Gaius. "You wouldn't need coffee to stay awake at night, with thoughts like that."

"It isn't a terrifying thought, though. It's a call to action." He turned to look at her. "With such a fleeting, exponentially small fraction of the universe to experience, knowing you won't leave a mark when all is said and done, what does that leave?"

"Now."

"Now, and the rest of your life. Live. Live for yourself. Enjoy that single note as if it was your song."

"Are you pushing me to run after Jet?"

He stood and his mood changed instantly. Frustration was clear in his voice. "The opposite. You have a close friend who understands your needs and desires here. Instead, you wonder if you will be happy, comfortable, or even alive if you run with Jet." He extended a hand to her. "You have your family. You have Iskendar. You can have me. Now and until the end of our lives."

"I know you can make me happy, Gaius." She looked at his hand and considered it as she spoke. "But what if—"

"'*If* is always going to be." He held the invitation of his hand still as he continued. "But what if I could make you happy now and always? I am your harmony, Hypatia."

Music started playing from somewhere out of sight.

Hypatia blushed and a smile leapt across her lips, lifting her cheeks and widening her eyes. Knowing he had planned the whole moment only made her appreciate it even more. "Oh Gaius," she said, taking his hand.

CHAPTER THIRTEEN

"You aren't naïve, Aeych." Jet was re-shelving a book. *Incorrectly, as usual,* Hypatia noted to herself. She had thought this was cute or endearing months ago, but she was now thoroughly tired of following in his disorganized wake. *It's not only Jet,* she thought. *Everyone does it.* Patrons of the Library messed up the order and she loved the order. Thinking this didn't dissipate her annoyance with him. She did always forgive Jet eventually. One look in those eyes and she was thinking about other things. "I'm here more often now, but my thoughts stray," he continued, not looking in her direction so he didn't notice her annoyance. "You know I could wright any minute and never return."

"You wouldn't do that. Not on purpose."

"I don't think I would right now. But the time that might change that could come."

They were researching for wrighting opportunities. Jet had given her tips. It was what he had come to Iskendar for in the first place. It was common to find him, when he wasn't looking for Hypatia, deep in the aisles of the Library, scanning pages and inadequately returning books to the shelves.

"You're right." Hypatia got up from the desk where she had stacked a series of books on flying. "Not about you leaving, but about me not being naïve. You won't change. You don't like change." She walked toward him as she spoke and pulled on his collar. "Look at these clothes. I don't think you've worn a different outfit."

"Clothes are scarce where I'm from."

"That's part of it." She pulled out the book he had shelved and placed it back correctly. "But you're attached to the look, too. The same style to your

62

hair, the same amount of stubble on your face—how do you even maintain it at such an odd but uniform length? And you wear the belt, pouch, tucked shirt and—" she reached for his necklace "—jewelry."

He deftly but gently redirected her hand before her fingers touched the pendant hanging around his neck, sliding her arm around his back instead. He brought her in close with his free hand. She laughed as he did, adding, "And the same tired moves."

"Tired? Bored with me already, Aeych?"

"Of course not." She leaned in close to kiss him, stopping short of his lips. They brushed close enough to feel the vibrations of energy pass between them. Opening her mouth slightly, she asked in a whisper, "Who is she?"

Jet jerked his head back at the question, a quizzical look on his face. Hypatia revealed no anger or jealousy, just curiosity and obviously more awareness than Jet had expected.

"Does it matter?" He smiled.

"Hmmm. I would guess it's not a romantic relationship. Otherwise you wouldn't wear such an obvious token."

"Maybe I would," he stammered.

Hypatia interpreted his surprise as an indicator of how close to the mark she was. "You don't handle guilt well, so I think that's not true." She ran her hand behind his head.

"I'm not one of your books. You can't read me like that."

"Not entirely," she mused, her eyes slowly moving across his face. "Enough, though. You are really good with secrets but terrible with emotions. Remind me to invite you to debate sometime. I could tear you down so easily." She lowered her eyes. "Too much emotion on your sleeve."

"I would be a fool to take you up on that."

"And I can tell I should stop asking you about the necklace."

"Thank you." He tilted his head, closed his eyes, and started inching his face toward her. "Can we get back to where we were?"

Her finger held back his lips. "First things first. Hand me that book you just put away."

Without letting her go, he pulled a weathered paperback from the shelf beside them and handed it to Hypatia. She reached past him and restored it to its place above and behind his head. As she created the order she loved so much, he kissed her. She thought as it happened, *This is weird. Weird and perfect.*

"Let's get out of here." She took his hand and led him toward the Library exit. Curiosity replaced the disappointment on his face. She smiled and continued to pull him along.

Suddenly Jet stopped and pulled her back in. "Where are we going?" he said with a cold curiosity.

She tore her hand from his and began running.

He chased her from the Library and followed her through the Capital. Her endurance was a bottomless well. The curiosity evolved into a game. She ran and so he followed. He was comfortable with the hunt. It held purpose.

They cleared the small outer buildings that marked the edges of the business centre of the Capital. She kept running, setting the pace and staying out of reach. They were now passing by the walled gardens of residences, all perfectly cared for and each as unique as the family that lived within. They followed a rough path toward a copse of trees. The descent out of the city levelled out, then started rising as they continued to run.

Jet glanced back as the last homes slipped into the distance behind them. He turned forward barely in time to avoid crashing into Hypatia.

"Whoa there."

Jet stopped suddenly and then had to lean forward to recover his breath. Hypatia, for all their activity, showed no signs of exertion.

"You seem like you could walk a long way without getting tired," she said. "I have never seen you out of breath before." Hypatia breathed with minimal difficulty and the light sheen of sweat on her skin made her glow in the fading light of the day. She noticed him staring and blushed.

Catching enough air to speak, he replied, "I'm more of a 'stand in one place, lift, repeat' sort of healthy." He gulped another breath. "There isn't a lot of room to walk, where I'm from."

"You don't talk about home."

"The mountains look closer from the city," Jet remarked, both in surprise at how far they had travelled and in an attempt to change the topic. "How much farther?"

Taking the cue, Hypatia turned toward the hills. "Technically we are already in the mountains. They've eroded away here to such an extent that the foothills we are in make up the base."

"How old are they?"

"As old as Iskendar. Their shape indicates they are truly older than any time even our Founders would have known." She grabbed his arm as he started walking toward a path leading into the forest. "Don't think I missed you changing the subject. I want to know more about the people in your world. Are mountains as old? Do you have founders?"

Jet swallowed and looked at her. "It's better to stick with talking about your world. Safer."

"Safe is boring." She leaned in close to him, brushing his neck with her nose. "I want danger and excitement. I want to be afraid. I want to have an adventure. I want to run."

He stroked her hair. "The chase isn't all you imagine it is."

"That's what you say, but I think—" She took off running.

Jet sighed and a smile tugged at the corner of his mouth. He took off after her again.

She moved fluidly through the trees. Fast and graceful, she darted along the pathway like she was a part of the environment. His running lacked the same fluidity but held its own grace and an impressive crashing, lumbering speed. Her dress disappeared from his view behind a rocky outcropping. Jet's feet pounded on the dirt and he puffed heavily as he rounded the rocks. He stopped suddenly.

Hypatia stood in the mouth of a cave only a few feet wide. She stared into the darkness. A wind was pulling the fabric of her dress in toward the opening as it also pushed it away. She spoke without turning, her voice reverberating in the cave making her sound imposing. "I want to stare into the dark. To be afraid."

"Fear isn't something you can put a stopper in. Sometimes what you find in the dark won't go back when you are done with it."

"I can run."

He approached her. "We can run. But always, eventually," he put his hand on her arm, "the darkness finds you. A brief look for you at first, but then the chaos and the evil never ends." He placed his other hand on her hip, tracing it along the small of her back and slowly turning Hypatia as he did. His arm turned to brace her back as his other hand pushed back her hair. She looked at him with warmth she'd never shown before.

"Jet will protect me."

"I will protect you. I will protect you from all that you fear. From all that you run from. From the dark." He kissed her.

The dampness of the cave cooled their bodies, overheated by the run. Breathing heavily, they traded exploring touches with their lips. Their hands clasped, and Hypatia pulled Jet toward her as she leaned back against the cave wall. They stayed there, balanced between the warmth of the fading summer day and the cold darkness of the underground.

CHAPTER FOURTEEN

That evening, long after Jet had left Iskendar, Hypatia sat watching the tiny waves expand in the garden pool, attempting to avoid eye contact with her mother. It was hard being the centred and authoritative Catalogue to the woman who had raised her. Her mother was the authority in the relationship for so long that changing roles felt like a battle for dominance in an awkward role-play.

"Books are doorways to other worlds." It was a vague, generic opening, but all she could think of. "Each page is a threshold to a new beginning or another ending."

"This sounds clichéd." Aurelia sounded stern.

"In a way, it's true," she continued, slightly deflated. "Some stories are doors for imagination. Others are . . ." She struggled with the description and then attempted a restart. "The words are pathways. Stones in a road like the cobblestone streets of Iskendar. Some pathways, some roads, are gateways." She was beginning to repeat herself; this wasn't starting well. "We can bridge those gates. Wright the words and the threshold appears." She thought for a moment. "Think of it as more of a slope you end up sliding down, then a gate."

"So you write the words out? Wouldn't that send the author of these passages to that other world? Writers would vanish on a regular basis."

"Not 'write' like putting words on a page. 'Wright' as in building. Like a shipwright, or . . ." She recalled her first discussion with Jet, wondering if her mother had the same thought process as her.

"So, how do you know how?"

"How what?"

"How to . . . *wright* the words? You obviously can't build a boat out of

66

them."

"You speak them."

"That's it? Speak them? So, again, my point remains the same. Wouldn't saying them out loud cause the speaker to disappear? Storytellers and writers are a most dangerous set of professions. A few wrong words, and *poof.*"

Hypatia mostly ignored her. "It's a combination of putting together the words that aren't normally paired, plus, I guess, conviction of thought."

"Explain." Aurelia switched tones effortlessly, moving now to her sternness with hints of annoyance and disappointment.

"When I have the correct passage I can see the path in my mind. When I speak the words, I see the road being built and the world, a snapshot, at the end of it."

"So." Hypatia was beginning to get annoyed at her mother's use of the word "so." She felt belittled by it. "So," Aurelia repeated, as if she knew doing so would annoy Hypatia, "you only have a snapshot."

"And a feeling."

"You are going to travel to another world on a feeling and a postcard."

"Basically."

"Okay, then."

"Okay?" Hypatia was surprised at her mother's response. "Okay like you are okay if I go?"

"Of course not. Not in a thousand lifetimes. This is dangerous, crazy, and reckless. I mean 'okay Hypatia, I get it.'" She casually said everything in a matter-of-fact way, closing all discussion.

"I'm going."

"No, you aren't." She used the same tone of closure, finality, that she used in any logical rebuttal. It occurred to Hypatia that her mother possessed her own alter ego as certain and as definite as The Catalogue. "You would throw away everything you've worked for your whole life. You would give up any respect you've earned. Frankly, I think you'd be giving up your life. We'd never see you again."

"I've done it before. It's safe," she said defiantly.

"Excuse me?" The cold tone was gone, replaced by raw anger and disgust. "You did this before?"

"Well, Jet did it." Her determination was suddenly on shaky ground. "And he took me."

"That's it. Jet. He's the reason. Jet this and Jet that. People are talking, you know."

"I know."

"And you are okay with it? The rumours?"

"Yes."

"And it affects your father and me as well."

"I never . . ." she stammered as the last of her confidence crumbled.

"And think of Gaius. He was so in love with you. Ready for a life with you."

Her argument left her and she lashed out in response. "That's his problem. This is my life."

"If you think that, then this conversation is over. You don't need my permission to throw your life away." Aurelia stood and walked into the house.

The breeze picked up and rippled across the pool.

Aurelia had a way of tearing down an argument that Hypatia never considered. A personal perspective that was full of emotion and maternal instinct. The Catalogue would always be at the mercy of emotions. It was histories, facts, and logic, but feelings could forego all of that. Aurelia was right, but Hypatia still knew which decision she was going to make.

She sat there staring at the place where her mother had been for several minutes.

Without saying a word, she put her face in her hands and wept.

CHAPTER FIFTEEN

Hypatia's argument with her mother began a stream of troubles.

When she woke the next day she found a request from Oren in the morning mail, demanding audience that afternoon. *It must have been hand delivered by a runner*, she thought. *This is serious.*

Worse still, her father had been the first to see the notice and was angrily stomping his frustrations around in the backyard. Hypatia could tell he had cleared a large area with nothing but an axe and disappointment. There would be a full flowerbed and accompanying feature by that evening if he held onto that anger.

Fearing his wrath, she finished her breakfast quickly, collected her things, and began a very long and solemn walk to the Capital, avoiding Gaius's shop. Her anxiety about the pending meeting, and because Jet had not appeared, made the day drag on. Hypatia alternated between distractedly assisting patrons and regularly checking every aisle for his appearance.

Following the long morning, she ignored eating any lunch and went straight from her work in the Library to the Capital offices. She was surprised that, even though she was early, the attendant led her into the mayor's office on arrival.

Staring awkwardly away from where Oren would be seated, not wanting to see the look on his face, she took a seat on the bench that, when she had last seen it, had been warming and inviting. Now it seemed isolated and cold.

"I will cut right to it." Hypatia looked up to see sullen disappointment on the mayor's face. She was not used to seeing that directed at her from anyone. "You know your responsibility as the Assistant to the Great

Librarian." Oren waved a hand toward Kalli, whom Hypatia had not expected to see there. "The events that happen now define your legacy."

It was not the kind of argument she would interrupt. She was being chastised.

"You have been seen interacting with the stranger for hours on end, in public and within the Library. To what end?"

She gave it some time and thought before she answered, "He seeks to save worlds, and our Library is the greatest resource he can access to achieve that goal."

"Perhaps it is The Catalogue he sees as the greatest resource," Kalli said in a low, insinuating voice. Her tone also suggested something more sinister, something that Hypatia had never heard from her before.

"Perhaps he does," Oren agreed. "And by what right should the stranger have access to any of the resources—or minds, for that matter—of Iskendar? Not that I believe our knowledge should be withheld—I agree it is best used for the good of the people. But more specifically, for the good of *our* people. I also fear that his presence and his research may put Iskendar in danger."

Hypatia remained silent. She knew there was no defendable argument. She didn't know what dangers Jet's wrighting presented for Iskendar. She felt confident that he would keep their safety in mind, but Jet had also said there was so much he didn't know about the enemy. *How could he protect Iskendar when worlds have fallen before him?*

"I resolve that you banish Jet from Iskendar until a committee can—"

"A committee?" She jumped up from her seat. "That will mean years before he can return."

"If he returns before he is summoned he will be imprisoned here. His means of wrighting, as you call it, will be stripped from him when that occurs. Then a committee of my choosing will be formed to discuss what is to be done with the stranger."

Hypatia wanted to scream at him, but bit her tongue.

"Kalli, do you agree?"

Kalli addressed Oren formally, "It is less a deterrent than what the Founders and what precedent would call for."

"I do not intend to send a message to people of other worlds," Oren said slowly, lost in thought. "I believe to act more rashly may in fact draw more attention to Iskendar and, in doing so, invite more of these strangers. Iskendar and its people are safer in isolation. Great Librarian, I ask that you please help to define and support this direction." Hypatia was intentionally being excluded now. She worried that this was going to be her future, her role a figurehead only.

Kalli replied in kind. "The course you decide in this matter will be justified, and I will back you."

"If the committee finds there is no danger from strangers coming to our world," Oren continued, "then you may call him back at such a time."

Hypatia knew no group of intellectuals from Iskendar would ever agree to this. She also knew that, with Kalli backing it, there would be no fighting this verdict.

"There is no way to call Jet. When he leaves he will not return." The words shot from her mouth. "We lose a great opportunity for gaining knowledge and expanding the strength of Iskendar. It must be on record that I believe the verdict to be incorrect."

Kalli stood. "It will not be recorded." This time her voice was forceful. "You are to be the Great Librarian. To defy officially the orders of this government and of your seated Great Librarian will divide our people. It is not acceptable."

"Agreed." Oren rubbed his hands together. "You may hold your opinions but we will not take them under advisement, nor keep any record of your dissenting voice. Kalli, I will relegate to you the responsibility of redefining The Catalogue's workload for the coming months. I believe she will be very busy for a long time."

"She will be." Kalli didn't smile, but she sounded pleased.

Hypatia was shuffled from the room, head down, after the others had left.

As she descended the stairs of the government offices, Hypatia noticed a group of young men and women huddled together and looking in her direction. One of the men, light haired, slender, and taller than Hypatia, was clearly the leader of the company. They were dressed casually in comparison to most denizens of the Capital, in light pants and t-shirts. The exception was their leader, who had commented to a smaller, dark-haired woman beside him and was now listening to her response. He was in full official political regalia and his expression held the same authority that his clothes proclaimed.

Hypatia understood, before they even moved, that a confrontation was imminent, serious, and inevitable. Expecting it and welcoming it, especially with how the day had been going, she strode defiantly toward the group's representative, sizing him up. He was younger than she had initially assumed, only a couple years past graduating from study. His posture, controlled and rigid, told her he'd been raised in a family of politicians, or at the very least, officially trained. She didn't recognize his face, which meant that he must not hold any public office. *At least not any office I have dealt with,* she thought.

She immediately recognized his name.

"Mamercus Aemilius Lepidus Livianus," he said, extending his hand.

Hypatia was about to speak, but he continued. "Office of Foreign Nations for the Medini Peninsula, and you are the Assistant to the Great Librarian, Hypatia Theon."

"You do me a disservice by not allowing me to deliver my own announcement." She wasn't actually upset, but realized she would need to take an upper hand early on, as the crowd would be against her in whatever Mamercus had planned.

"Hypatia Theon needs no identification, and her reputation is only her own to harm."

She suspected his argument was going to be about Jet when he said this. The man was mimicking an article that had appeared in the Capital's gossip news.

"Thank you." She would have to take the high road; keeping him under her thumb would be difficult. "I recognize both your name and title as diplomat. You have done great work, most recently with the negotiation of trade agreements between Medini and the people of Arisa, to your north. I particularly like your provision to divide all the, what did you call it? *Crumbs* for those who did the hard work of serving the food." Hypatia knew the provision was added to impress upon the workers of Arisa that Medini considered itself an entitled nation.

"I am not here to discuss my own success or receive your praise," —if he was impressed at her ability to recall the small details of his diplomacy, he hid it well— "as valuable as it might be these days." *He is taking the low road*, she thought. "It is relevant, though, that you mention my recent work with Arisa, as in that region, rumour places your stranger." He drew out the words, understanding the negative impact it would have on her and noticing her shift uncomfortably as he said it.

"His name is Jet," she said in reaction to the word "stranger." It was an uncalculated thing to say and he might be getting under her skin, she thought. Oren had called him stranger too often for her liking.

"I am glad we are on the same topic." He glanced around to members of his group, who were getting excited and nodding in agreement.

Hypatia settled into The Catalogue, knowing that Mamercus was walking into a fight he could not win. "I do see where this is going." She drew up her sleeves and stepped into the street, leading him. "I'll give you audience to make your argument. Then you can watch as I tear it down before you."

He confidently followed her onto the street, his group trailing closely behind. "Your providing this opportunity is recognized. But, as you will see, the argument will hold true in both initial delivery and under scrutiny. Withstanding all of your rebuttal, there will be no tearing down, for the walls I build are those you built. To tear them down is to undo yourself."

72

The group clapped and he smiled and feigned an attempt to quiet them.

She had seen this approach before and had seen it done well. The clapping had brought the attention of others.

"We do not have the extensive libraries, the vast collection of volumes available in the Capital in Medini. You must derive your current course from some doctrine available due to your more civilized education."

He's playing the small town, simple fool overshadowed and envious of my privileged place, she thought. *That's defensible.*

"The doctrine I follow," she started, directing her words at the gathering crowd, knowing they were the ones to win over, "is the guiding principle of Iskendar. In all I do, that is the commandment with which I stay grounded. Surely in Medini the same statement of value applies."

A fire lit up in his eyes that suggested that she was playing into his trap. "The mission—no, the vision" —he was directing his words to his own entourage— "of the people in Medini is guided by those commandments and connected to Iskandar. We agree. Then, Hypatia Theon, Assistant to the Great Librarian, enlighten us as to which commandment applies to your choice to accept this stranger. What word of the Founders says to embrace the clearly forbidden abandonment of technology that has been witnessed in his vanishing?"

He was baiting her. There was no commandment that she could present that would not immediately be thrown back in her face. She would need to redirect the assumption.

"Jet" —*give him a name*, she thought, *it will soften the concept*— "uses an ability that is not technological. It neither violates nor aligns with our most sacred of rules. This was not progress. When a flower grows in your garden that you have never seen before, do you fear it? It was discovered, not developed."

"When I find a weed, I pull it. Those weeds, even those of the least invasive kind, can ruin your garden."

Ouch, well played, she thought. "A weed is a flower whose purpose no one has yet understood. Once you've decided it doesn't belong, this new flower needs to be studied." It felt weird referring to Jet as a flower.

"Studied by committee with peer review."

"And while we wait, the weed, the potential flower, dies."

"Pull the weed and study the dead remains then, I say." His tone became almost sarcastic. "But you, Hypatia, study the weeds by joining them in the garden, oblivious to their spreading poison."

"Instead you would destroy the future of trade? Of discovery? Of beneficial relationships? And we lose the potential understanding of our history."

He moved toward her. "I put forth that the safety of our people is more important than that potential."

"More important than Jet's life."

"Indeed, more important than any one life. The Founders made it clear that society is the core. The people mean everything. The stranger means the end of Iskendar."

She was raging inside but she maintained her calm demeanour. "You cut off one person and you think the problem is fixed? In Medini is weeding so easy? Do your farmers only deal with a single blight in their fields? To work in such easy conditions must be sweet. Do you regard the farmers in Medini or Arisa as lacking in hard work?"

"They work." His voice sounded strained; his confidence was slipping. "Their fields are full of weeds."

"Full, you say? Perhaps someone important should help there. I could recommend some advisors that would be glad to share programs that have been successful in other communities. The Library has references to—"

"So we get to the heart of the infestation," he cut in, out of turn. "You let a stranger into our most treasured resource. Allow him free access."

"Like anyone on Iskendar."

"Like anyone *of* Iskendar." He nearly spat the words out. Approaching her aggressively, he continued. "He has no right to our knowledge. He taints it with his uncultured presence."

"Jet is not uncultured."

"He poisons our words with his magic."

She stepped toward him. "He is not poison." Her anger would be read as unwilling to back down.

He pointed a finger at her, so close to her face that she wanted to bite it off. "Even the potential Great Librarian is infected by his disease. So much that she violates the very foundations of Iskendar."

Disease? Poison? He was making this personal. She was going to ruthlessly tear him down. He was on the ropes and lashing out. Now he was ripe; she would ruin him.

Hypatia opened her mouth to speak and Jet's voice came out.

"Hey guy, leave her alone! She is not infected by anything. I don't infect things. And you don't get any diseases from wrighting."

She spun on her toes to see Jet stomping across the street. He was reaching over his shoulder to pull something from his pack. He produced a pair of wooden sticks nearly the length of his forearm. They were wrapped in cloth at one end, where he gripped them. He pointed one at Mamercus and shouted, "Step back from her or I will hurt you."

Shocked, obviously never having been in a physical altercation, Mamercus jumped back and shielded his face. "Don't hit me!"

"Jet, what are you doing?" Hypatia had recovered from her surprise and was now turning her anger previously directed at Mamercus on Jet instead. "Get back!" She placed her hands on his chest and shoved him back. "What are those, weapons?"

"These are my canne." He came forward again. "And if he is threatening you, I will break him."

"We do not fight on Iskendar."

Mamercus seized on Hypatia's words. "The stranger does not understand anything but violence and destruction. The stranger will hurt us all—*kill* us all."

"He is not familiar," Hypatia attempted to shout back, but the crowd picked up on his suggestion quickly. Seeing Jet's enraged face and how intense his posture was helped to turn this crowd against him.

Jet was the stranger to them.

Hypatia was blindsided by her sudden isolation. She understood what they saw in him and how they felt it was impacting her. The Great Librarian was a role model to the people, a figure of cultured authority, and she was now functioning far outside of that expectation.

Striding past Jet, she headed toward her home without looking back. Moments later she heard the heavy boots of the man Iskendar viewed as the stranger catching up to hers. The strength, the weight of the sound was so foreign that Hypatia tensed as he approached.

"I'm sorry," he said, breathing heavily, "clearly that isn't how things are done here." He was keeping pace but not walking too close to her.

They walked quickly, just short of running. Hypatia was focused. She was going home and then they were leaving.

They were going to wright.

75

CHAPTER SIXTEEN

Jet didn't speak again until they left the busy city core. "Hypatia, listen. I reacted." He walked up beside her and Hypatia slowed her pace slightly to match his. "I feel protective of you and sometimes I just jump into a situation without thinking."

"Without knowing," Hypatia said, not looking at him.

"I guess, but I don't really see the difference."

"On Iskendar you act when you know. Thinking comes automatically for everyone. Even for you, despite what those people think. Once you have turned your thoughts to something then you can know the course of action." It seemed a smaller distinction when she said it out loud, but she felt it was important.

"Alright, I acted without knowing what I was getting into or what I was doing."

"We need to learn, understand, and react when all known possibilities have been examined. This is the way of Iskendar. The way of my people."

"I get it. I'm sorry."

"I don't want you sorry, I want you prepared." She stopped now and took his arm, "You need to know how I think. I need your support if we are going to wright together."

His face looked like he had been slapped. Recovering, he moved to speak and then, clearly thinking on the lesson Hypatia had just imparted, thought about what he needed to say. Taking long enough to demonstrate he was thinking but not changing his thought, he finally responded, "If I am to keep you safe and supported, I can only do that here."

"I've had enough of here. Can't you see that?"

"You have no idea—"

"I've seen it, Jet."

"You've seen it?"

"Regen."

Jet had to stop to think on the word. "What is Regen?"

"Regen is not a what, it's a where. It's where we're going." She turned away from him and took his hand as they started walking again. "Have you ever wanted to see an endless sunshine?" He didn't respond immediately and she continued. "I've seen ships. Massive wooden structures larger than the buildings on Iskendar, with sails three times the height of their hull. Driven forward on the strongest winds across a desert."

"How do ships move on a desert?"

"I don't know. But I want to know and I found the words to get there."

"You're sure? When did you have time to look?"

"It's all in here already," she said, tapping the side of her head, "and these gates come together on their own. Regen has been the clearest. I can see the words that make the gate a new world shining brightly at the end."

Chasms of existence leave gaping holes in the flesh.

"We don't know what's there, or if 'there' still exists."

"I don't care. I need to go. Regen is calling to me and Iskendar is pushing us away," she said, looking off into the distance.

"I can't take you, Aeych. I'm scared that only death or worse will be waiting there. And if your plan is to wright away from Iskendar, then where are we walking to?"

"Home. Once more, in case I never see it again."

"I won't take you," he said, his voice stern.

Her focus was unbreakable. "I'm going, Jet. If you don't come, I'll do it alone. Your choice isn't keeping me here or letting me go. Your decision is only this: do we go together?"

"Of course. I will follow you anywhere. But Aeych, I will use everything in my power to keep you here."

"I know, but I have the words and unless you remove my tongue I am destined for Regen."

They walked into her garden as she finished and Hypatia slowed. She wanted to take it all in as they made their way to the house.

No one was inside. "I was hoping my parents would be here, but it looks like they've gone out. I'll leave them a note." She took a pen from the table and found a scrap of paper. "I feel like a runaway child." She shook her head, trying to dispel a little of her excitement, fear, and nervousness. "I sound like one too. Great," she added sarcastically.

Jet said nothing as he watched her write a few words on the scrap, then bend and tighten her sandals. She wrapped an additional belt around her dress to pull in some of the flowing fabric, then looked at him. "Ready?" she asked as she pulled up her hair.

"Now? That's it?"

"Yes, it is. Hold onto me." Hypatia wrapped her arms around him.

"This feels a bit backwards," Jet tried to say.

She hushed him, hugged him close, and kissed him once quickly. Looking into his eyes, she spoke the words, imagining the path before her opening up. "Chasms of existence leave gaping holes in the flesh."

The Catalogue laid bare her mind and Regen came flooding in.

* * *

In the garden behind the house, Quint was startled by the sound of rushing wind and paper. He turned just in time to see an extending vertical line of light, and a bright flash. He ran into the kitchen and found Hypatia's scrap now on the floor. He bent and picked it up.

Thank you for everything. I hope to see you again someday. Until then, know I love you and that you made my dreams here possible.

She had signed it with her full name but with no title.

CHAPTER SEVENTEEN

As Hypatia uttered the words she could feel the wind whipping up around them. Pages were turning and the world was slipping away.

The fluttering noise gathered just as it had when Jet took her away from Iskendar before. The rushing and crashing of a thousand pages filled their ears. The sound reached a crescendo and they were swept off their feet.

Silence.

It felt like falling.

Then the rushing sound of wind shot back in around them. The world became blindingly bright and hot. Opening her eyes, Hypatia took in an endless blue sky.

Panic set in as it dawned on Hypatia that the world wasn't slipping away. They were free-falling.

Jet screamed something she was unable to make out. Reacting, Hypatia grabbed him tightly and they began to spiral downward. The air rushed up toward them and simultaneously pushed them sideways. She closed her eyes in fear, to make the world disappear, but that made the spinning and tumbling as they plummeted worse. She would have felt sick if the panic wasn't overwhelming her. Jet's heart was beating hard against her, matched by her own heart, beating as if to burst from her chest.

They fell and fell. Jet was still screaming, the words lost to the wind.

Hypatia barely made out the word "ship" as Jet yelled and she attempted to grip him closer. As she moved her hand away from his side, the wind forced her whole arm away. Jet started to push against her, sliding his feet between them. She could tell he was trying something. She opened her eyes in time to see a massive shadow, dark brown, coming toward them at a ridiculous pace. *Or are we moving toward it?*

Before another thought formed, they struck the ship. Jet's back hit it first and Hypatia tumbled onto a railing before slamming hard to the deck. The back of her skull smacked on wood. A bright white star leapt into her vision. As the brightness faded she could see Jet, standing weakly, go limp then tumble over the rail on the edge of the ship. She reached toward him, trying to push to her feet with her other hand. "No!" she tried to scream, but all the power had left her lungs.

A crash, the thud of heavy footfalls behind her, and suddenly her wrist was lashed to the railing Jet had just tumbled over; in a single swift movement, someone had gripped her arm and secured it to the vessel's railing. Hypatia glimpsed red hair and dark clothes as someone launched themselves over the side. Had she imagined that? She could swear the mysterious person had been pulling down a pair of goggles as they dove.

Then the world went dark.

CHAPTER EIGHTEEN

Hypatia woke on a cot. Voices were chattering excitedly around her.

"What happened? Jet?" Hearing her own voice surprised her.

"He's out still," someone said—a man. "A little shock, is all. He isn't hurt."

Hypatia's eyes shot open at the unfamiliar accent.

A man stood there. His skin was tanned dark, far beyond that of the farmers who tended their fields outside the Capital. He wore tighter clothing than them, and despite being quite muscular, he was also very slim. Hypatia could only describe it as sturdy looking.

"My name is Chezpa," the man said, and held out a hand. "If you are still too tired I do not expect you to shake it."

Hypatia sat up quickly, looking past Chezpa, taking in her surroundings. The room resembled the inside of a cargo ship. Cots filled the room—several rows in the centre with others lining the sloped walls on all sides. The beds were stacked in twos and each had a curtain and side table. A low, rumbling hum came from all around her.

Distractedly she took Chezpa's hand. His grip was firm and her own hand felt crushed under the strength of it. Hypatia squeaked slightly as he shook it.

"This is my crew," he said, letting go of her hand to gesture to the throng of people behind him. All of them were dressed the same, in tight leathers that appeared protective, but more like work clothes than armour. Most had head coverings with shaggy hair of all kinds protruding from the edges. Chezpa continued. "You are on the *Husak*. First question, how did you get here?"

"The Husak? What's a Husak?"

Chezpa's eyebrows rose. "You have not heard of the *Husak*? How is it possible you have not heard of one of the fleet? One of the best of the fleet, I might add." The gathered group heartily agreed. "You are not so young that you have never encountered all of the fleet, or at the very least not learned all the names."

"I'm not from here."

"Well obviously, as you are not a crew member. Which ship do you come from?"

"Wait, there's a better question." This was a girl's voice. Hypatia turned her head toward it and saw her sitting on a bunk several feet away. "How'd ya get all the way here? Where's your lari and how'd you manage to get two of you this far?" There was something familiar about the girl. Hypatia's memory dragged forth the image of the person leaping from the ship after Jet. She sounded younger than Hypatia but her skin made her look older. Like everyone else in the crew, her skin was dark. Her hair was a shocking red.

"What's a lari, and . . ." Hypatia stopped, understanding answering this question was pointless, and changed tack. "I'm not from this world."

Those in the crowd looked around at each other and a few laughed, as if they thought this was a joke but weren't sure how it would be funny.

Jet stirred and grunted a little at the commotion.

"This is Jet and I am Hypatia Theon," she said, and tried to stand up, but she was still dizzy from the fall and hitting her head. Reaching back, she rubbed a sizable bump on her scalp and winced. She sank back down onto the cot and continued. "I am from Iskendar and Jet is my companion. We travelled to Regen by wrighting."

"Like writing a book?" Chezpa asked.

"That explains it," the girl chimed in. "She's an intellectual with all the reading and writing. She's never heard of the Husak because she's ne'r lifted her head from a book."

A few crew members laughed at this. The girl, enjoying the attention her joke had garnered, pushed back her tangled red hair and adjusted her goggles.

"Meeko, please," Chezpa chided. "Even an intellectual would know of the Husak and all the other ships on Regen."

Jet, still shaky from the fall as well, spoke without lifting his head. "She is telling the truth. We're from another world. We came here by using gates that can transport us unbelievable distances. Hypatia and I are even from different worlds from each other."

"You need rest," Chezpa said. "Get some now and we will speak again over dinner." He addressed the crew. "Everyone back to work." They filed out the closest hatchway.

Hypatia thought rest was a great idea.

"You're going to let her sleep on my cot?"

"Meeko, again, please relax," Chezpa said as he pushed her out an open hatchway.

Hypatia looked at Jet, who had a smile on his face that said two things at the same time: *I am so happy you are alive* and *I was right*. They fell asleep together, Jet's hand on her shoulder.

* * *

When Hypatia woke, Meeko was hovering over the still sleeping Jet. "Oh, he is a good-looking fellow, isn't he?" she said, obviously aware that Hypatia was awake. "Do you all have such soft skin on your world?"

"Yes. Compared to my aged father, his skin is dried leather."

"So, this hunk is from another world than yours?"

Meeko wouldn't take her eyes off of Jet and it made Hypatia feel something new. "Yes, but he's with me and we came to Regen together."

"I hear you loud and I hear you clear." Meeko moved over to one of the double cots and jumped up to sit on the upper cot. "But let's say if anything happens to ya, maybe I could travel with Jet."

"Are the people of Regen always so rude?"

"Life's short. Get while you can."

Jet opened his eyes and sat straight up. "Aeych?"

"My name's Meeko," she said, stealing his attention. "The captain, who I will have ya know is my father, has asked that I show ya round when yer up. Looks like yer up." She jumped down from the cot. "Let's go." She headed to the hatchway without waiting for them, popped it open, and slipped through. She was out of sight before the two travellers could rise.

Hypatia and Jet took the time to get their bearings and tentatively stand. The moment they were both steady, he embraced her. Hypatia almost fell back down, still dizzy.

Meeko was waiting in the hall for them. "We're on one of the lowest levels so there isn't so much wind noise in here."

Hypatia had noticed the constant rumble was still present, felt as much as heard. The noise was part of the world, noted only on a subliminal level by its occupants.

"My father thinks that, since ya clearly took none of the safety precautions before coming to Regen, ya have no idea where ya are."

"He believes us, then?" Jet asked, rubbing his head.

"How'd he do anything else? You fell from the sky."

"Maybe we came from another ship," Hypatia added, trying to be helpful.

83

"None in sight."

"Well, perhaps there were some clouds or a swell that the other ship was behind." Hypatia couldn't understand why there wouldn't be a plausible reason that would explain their arrival to the crew.

"No idea what a swell is, unless ya mean this vessel is swell. You sure as heck weren't hiding behind the Husak. We saw the two of ya dropping from the sky. Lucky I was working on the deck."

"You saved us?" Jet asked.

"I saw her go over the rail for you," Hypatia said as they followed Meeko into a room at the end of the narrow hallway. She held the hatch as they entered.

"It was nothing, really. Easy peasy. But ya can thank me later if ya like." Meeko smacked Jet's behind as he passed. Hypatia felt a little bile rise in the back of her throat.

Closing the hatch, Meeko crossed the room to a large door and several mechanical devices. Hypatia noticed the rumble was louder in this room and she felt far less stable.

"Let me show ya what Regen is." Meeko said this with a flourish of her hand toward a large lever. She leaned her entire weight on the metal rod, which protruded from a metal box attached to the wooden wall of the ship. Grasping it with both hands, she jumped up slightly. This was either to add the weight needed to get it going or, more likely, to add additional drama to the display.

The screech of grinding gears filled the room, loud enough to overwhelm the ever-present noise of the wind. When the lever reached the deck, a hatch behind Meeko cracked open. She let go of the handle and behind the walls, gears and pulleys could be heard fighting into motion. The hatch continued to open and Meeko slid on her goggles. The wind began whipping her wild red hair.

The light from the open sky and the wind crashed in to greet them.

It took a few attempts of blinking back tears and squinting for Hypatia's eyes to adjust to the brightness. Her ears hurt as all the air seemed to be sucked from the bay. Rushing wind was the only sound they could hear and the only thing they could see was sky. No desert, no ocean, no ground.

This ship was flying.

Meeko flipped a spyglass off a hook on the wall and tossed it to Jet with an unnecessary amount of flair. Hypatia could barely make out the word "Bly" as Meeko shouted and pointed out the hatch into the distance.

Staring into the endless sky hurt Hypatia's eyes, even though they had adjusted to most of the light shining in from the opening. From the look of the clouds and the tiny specks below them, which must have been part of the landscape, Hypatia could tell they were looking out the rear of the vessel and that it was moving fast. Really fast.

Blinking back more tears, she was able to make out a large, blackish-brown blob in the distance. It was gliding up and down, travelling at nearly the same speed as the Husak. She looked over at Jet, who had lowered the telescope with a look of disbelief on his face, only to raise it back up. He was trying to reconcile what was in the distance with the image in the glass.

He handed the spyglass to Hypatia and, as she raised it to her eye, she noticed Meeko smiling slyly, pleased that she was getting the reaction she had hoped for.

Finding the blob against the bright blue sky was easy.

"Rabbits?" she said out loud, but though they resembled rabbits, they were nearly four times the size of the rabbits on Iskendar. She noticed the claws next. They were long and sharp, and reflected the sunlight. Enormous ears seemed to act as sails, keeping the creatures lifted on the wind. They were all ears, fierce claws, and the cutest bunny faces she had ever seen. Yet, as hard as that was for her to comprehend, it wasn't the most impressive part. There were hundreds of them. Somehow they were flying in tandem. The rabbits, or blys, as Meeko had shouted, were linked together by a force Hypatia was unable to see. If they would come closer, she'd be able to tell how they did it. The telescope was decent, but nothing like the ones back in the Capital.

She lowered the spyglass and Meeko kicked the lowered lever, jolting it back into place. The gears and pulleys whirred again, drowning out the wind. The hatch slid firmly closed, cutting off the wind and leaving the bay suddenly silent, though the rushing air still raged against the hull outside. It took a moment for their ears to adjust to the change in pressure.

"Blys," Meeko said proudly.

"Where is the ground here? What do they eat?" Jet asked eagerly. "Do they just fly around all the time? Are they dangerous?" His curiosity was greater than she had ever seen it on Iskendar.

Meeko was very happy to entertain all of his questions. "They aren't dangerous," she said, and set her goggles back up on her head. "They eat the flowers and greens that we grow. My father says they were once stowaways and pests on ships, generations ago. He also says they were such a problem that the things were thrown overboard by the armload. That was before they could fly."

"Oh, that sounds just horrible," Hypatia said.

Meeko continued, unbothered. "Yeah, well, maybe. Things were harsher in the back-then. Root harvesting was way harder before the farms were built and the stupid things made it worse."

"Farms? How do you farm on this place? Is there some ground?" Jet was still alight with curiosity and Hypatia was taking it as a personal insult.

How could Regen be more exciting than Iskendar? And Jet was *her* stranger.

"Oh there is ground, alright. Ya go to ground when ya die. Everything dies down there. Everything goes to ground eventually, too. Too much wind and the rocks, and the sand and the spires and the debris."

"Then how do you farm?"

"Ye're on one." Meeko smiled again, with more pride even than when she showed them the blys. "Follow me."

Meeko took them toward the front of the ship. As they moved through the rooms, Hypatia began to get a sense of how huge the flying vessel really was. They went through a room made for storage. This was nearest the room with the hatch that they had just left. It branched off into other storage areas where Hypatia could make out large baskets full of some sort of fruit, crates, and a variety of long tools that were strapped to the walls. Other storerooms were empty, probably waiting for goods to be stored once produced.

Meeko swung open a heavy door and they entered a common area, with two tables on either side of a ladder that rose from the middle of the room. The tables could easily seat ten people each. The room was lit by electric lamps strung along the ceiling. They crossed this area and Meeko pushed open another heavy door. Now they were in the sleeping quarters.

Seeing the area now that her dizziness had subsided, Hypatia realized just how cramped the space was—probably made more so by the beds filling the room from end to end. Hypatia estimated there were about fifty beds, all in varying states of tidiness. It was crowded, but the area around each cot seemed to be personalized by the owners, who breathed some unique part of themselves into the space. Sketched images, trinkets, scattered clothing, storage containers, and other random items made each space unique. A few even looked like shared quarters, spaces shared by a couple or maybe even small families.

Exiting that room, they walked down a hallway that led to a single metal door. A sign clearly warned *NO FLAMES. NO BLYS. NO SICKNESS.* There was a handle on it similar to the hatch lever, but it twisted sideways instead of cranking up or down.

"It's more impressive if ya go first." Meeko pointed at the door. "Jet?"

Hypatia shot a glance at Meeko, who pretended not to see it.

Jet grabbed the heavy handle and turned it sideways. It creaked like the mechanics in the hatch room, but it wasn't automatic so he had to pull heavily to swing it open. Jet stepped back and invited Hypatia to enter first. "Aeych?"

Hypatia smiled and felt embarrassed for getting jealous, but also hoped Meeko felt smaller and less sure at the gesture.

She stepped through the hatchway onto a metal balcony. There were stairs on both sides, one heading up and the other down. A slight breeze raised goosebumps on her arms and ruffled her hair in a playful way. She looked up, "They must go up at least four levels."

Jet stepped out after her. His jaw dropped open.

"And down four more, as well," Meeko added as she slid in behind Jet.

Each level had a platform that led up to a patch of thick roots. The roots intertwined and extended from the bottom to the top of the massive vault. By the angles of the wooden frame construction, Hypatia could tell this was the front of the ship. Cracks of light came in between the roots in places as the plant or plants appeared to be anchored by a thousand arms that extended outside the wall.

Green pods hung from the roots. They looked like giant seeds. The stems that held them ranged in length from a foot to over ten feet. They were swaying with the movement of the ship and the constant exchange of air that was taking place between the roots of the plants.

"We call 'em babs." Meeko deftly twisted a pod from a stem; it looked very ripe, as far as Hypatia could tell. "The fruit's kind of dry but the roots extract the water from the atmosphere outside and make it possible for us to collect it." She pulled a tool from her belt that looked like a blunted knife and struck the bab fruit. It cracked from top to bottom. She pulled it apart and displayed the white flesh, which looked like pieces of curdled cheese, but drier.

Meeko turned away from them and tipped a small covered bucket that was hanging from the nearest root. Water poured into one of the bab fruit halves, which Meeko promptly stirred with her finger. "This'll be kind of raw still. We haven't done any of the prep with it." She handed half the pod to Jet and added water to the other.

Jet put a little in his mouth and started to chew. The curious expression he had maintained throughout their tour through the farm ship quickly pinched into a pucker.

"Yeah, it's pretty sour, too." Meeko laughed as Jet struggled with the flavour and Hypatia couldn't help but laugh as well. Jet's facial contortions squished his face and brought out even his thinnest stress lines. "This is a root farm. It's what the Husak was built for."

"It's huge," Hypatia said as she swept her gaze from the top to the bottom of the chamber in an attempt to take it all in.

"This is one of the smallest farms, but we are the best," Meeko said. "Ye've got the miners that harvest the metal from the spires, but they're smaller. The *Arcadia* is ten times bigger than the *Husak*."

Hypatia perked up. "You have a ship called the *Arcadia?*" *Could this have something to do with the Founders of Iskendar?* She thought it must be related. *But how? Iskendar is billions of worlds away.*

"Yeah. Arcadia's the oldest ship. If ya believe the old folks, it's been flying for ten thousand generations. It's so big they use it ta build all the other ships."

"How many ships are there?"

"Eighteen at last count. Ya can't always be sure. We usually get reports from anyone ya might meet up with or trade with. Could be there's nineteen ships out there, if ya ignore news that the *Naus* went to ground. We heard from the *Mehvea*, but they're always crazy with the gossip. Nothing else to do, I guess."

Meeko gave them some time to explore the rest of the farm, always sticking close to Jet. He and Hypatia were awestruck by all that they saw.

"Now ya've seen the ship—the lower parts, anyways. Cap'n wants to give ya some work. Earn yer keep, if ya plan on staying."

Hypatia did plan on staying. She had no desire to return home.

CHAPTER NINETEEN

Learning to harvest the bab fruits was easy for Jet. Hypatia could tell that he was accustomed to the hard labour and long days of climbing branches, tossing down fruits, and carting them to the storage areas. He had the strength for lifting the roots and the endurance for collecting the water buckets. Jet also showed a secret talent for helping to hunt the blys. Hypatia had been too afraid to try and even more afraid to watch him hunt, because she didn't really want to know what danger he might be in.

Hypatia, for her part, was adept at adjusting the grow rails for the roots. Directing growth through the use of grow rails was vital on the farm. Proper distribution of weight was critical to keep tons of lumber, metal, and people aloft on a world under a constant gale. The massive bab roots had to be controlled in their patterns and paths of growth.

The balancer, a man named Guri, set the rules for root growth, resource storage, and harvesting. He even managed specific bunk placement, bunk assignments, and individual sleeping schedules.

Hypatia guessed they had been on Regen for nearly three weeks. Guri had put Jet in the same double bunk assignment as Hypatia. They were also in the same sleeping schedule. Work shifts could happen at any time, as the length of a day was very hard to measure, with the constant movement over Regen. This timing made Hypatia tired for the first week—she spent long "nights" restlessly trying to sleep, then dragging herself from bed feeling listless and unrested. Now she was used to it.

Jet had been spending more time with her off-shift. The trade of sleep for Jet was worth it. She was infatuated with him and every moment they could have together was an infinite pleasure. Intimacy, though, came with minimal privacy on the ship. Each bunk had a curtain to surround a single cot only. It was pinned back to the posts when not in use and could be clipped shut when needed to avoid giving a free view to those in nearby bunk assignments. The curtains were terrible at muffling sound. This meant they had to be very quiet, a discretion not normally observed by others— and, occasionally, ignored in the passion of the moment by Jet and Hypatia.

Due to a particularly late night of muffled passion, Hypatia was having a hard time wrapping the guide wire around a small, awkwardly shaped root. "What I wouldn't give for a coffee," she mumbled to herself.

The plan for the next two weeks, as laid out by Guri, was to extend the tiny one-inch diameter root sixty-five degrees to port and ten degrees more than the current trajectory from ground level. The balancer had been especially concerned that the preceding two months had been wetter, and the increased moisture meant increased growth. Hypatia had a hard time telling wet periods from dry periods when they had originally arrived. After three weeks on Regen, she could sense the difference. It wasn't in the air; it was in the dampness of her skin, the dryness of her eyes, the amount of perspiration Jet was covered in when he collapsed on the bunk at end of their shift. As she thought about it, the smell of his sweat crept into her nose.

"How is it going, beautiful?"

In the dryness and constant heat of this world, she rarely thought of herself as beautiful. It lifted her spirits to hear Jet's voice, but she immediately thought of her appearance. Food was sparse, especially compared to the indulgences of Iskendar. Hypatia had become significantly thinner—not skeletal, but leaner, more muscular, and less well-fed. The labour was intense at least and crushing at its worst. She missed study, books, gardens, and the variety of faces she would see on a given day in the Capital. On the Husak there was a crew of forty, and day over day you would see every one of them, repeatedly.

"We can't stay here forever." She didn't look up. She was working on the last tie-off.

"I've been thinking the same thing. I need to take you home."

She paused at the idea of home before replying, "I don't think it will feel like home anymore. A lot of people will be unhappy." Dusting off her hands, she stood up and surveyed her work. She felt pride at a job well done in her one-foot square workspace. "I might have to make it up. My post has been vacant all this time."

"Don't worry about it, Aeych. Someone else will fill in for you."

"My position is for life. I disappeared. I didn't die. No one can replace me like that."

"A whole planet feels the same as me? Well, that's some serious competition for your affections. Could make a man jealous."

"Don't be smart. You know my home is with you." She wrapped her arms around him and laid her head on his chest. "Wherever you and I go, I'm home."

He ran his hands through her hair without speaking. It was enough for Hypatia to understand he felt the same.

Shouts came down from above. Meeko was calling Jet for something.

Hypatia instinctively winced at the sound and sighed demonstratively. Weeks aboard the ship, working closely with her, had done nothing to improve the relationship they had. Hypatia tried to tell herself her dislike didn't stem from jealousy, but she couldn't help physically reacting whenever Meeko called his name.

"Jet!"

On cue, Hypatia winced again.

"We'll go back to Iskendar soon. I'm ready when you are," he said, ignoring Meeko's shouts.

"Jet!"

"Now? Can we go now?" Hypatia asked, only half joking.

He laughed, "She's not your competition. If you could get over that, I think you two would be friends."

"Jet! Come on!"

Hypatia winced again. "I doubt it."

"Let's go see what's up." He took her hand and they ascended the stairs that rose alongside the bab tree. Hypatia marked in her mind all the branches she had worked on, counting nearly a hundred before they reached the top of the four flights. Almost a hundred coils in all those weeks, and the oldest had grown less than an inch, she noticed.

"Hurry up! We're going to miss it." Meeko bolted through the door as she spoke.

Jet let go of Hypatia's hand to fit through the doorway and hurried after her. Disappointed, Hypatia followed quickly, thinking how her robes from Iskendar would get caught up in the inner workings, the doorways, and the exposed bolts of the Husak. Her "Regen clothes," as she called them, were made of woven leather that was light and form-fitting. It made slipping down the hallways and working easier. They were utilitarian. Like everything on Regen, they reminded her of work. Even eating was a chore that required constantly adding measured amounts of water to create a nearly palatable paste.

Distracted in thought, Hypatia was caught by surprise when a pair of goggles were thrown her way. They struck her face and clattered to the floor. "Catch!" shouted Meeko sarcastically. She was dressed in her full deckside gear, complete with her lari, the flying device she had used to save Jet when they'd arrived.

Hypatia rubbed her face where the goggles had connected. "I can always count on you being mature."

"I can always count on you being distracted," retorted Meeko. "Yer head is always somewhere else." Her smile was more like a sneer. "Be careful ya don't lose sight of Jet, or someone might sneak him away when yer busy thinking."

"Thankfully, at least one of us is capable of thinking."

"Ooh, that cuts deep."

Hypatia was a little pleased that Meeko didn't have a comeback. Every conversation was a sparring match that Hypatia wanted badly to win. On Regen Hypatia was at a severe disadvantage in groups with Meeko. She could leverage Regen-specific insults and win the crowd over. Back home Hypatia could always count on the knowledge and resources about Iskandar that were at her disposal. Back home.

"For the last time, both of you, cut it out," Jet said. "Meeko, apologize."

She looked at Hypatia and twisted her sarcastic smile into an apologetic pout, complete with sad eyes. She turned to Jet. "Ye're right, Jet." Hypatia winced. "It was mean." She turned back to face Hypatia. The pout was gone, replaced by the sarcastic smile. "Sorry." It sounded sincere, but the defiant look belied it.

Not knowing what else to do, Hypatia quickly stuck her tongue out and put on her goggles.

Jet sighed. "Aeych."

Meeko's smile widened. She followed it up by reaching to a port window on the back wall of the ship. She flipped a screw and pulled back a small handle connected to it and it came unsealed. Wind rushed in and the air was sucked out and replaced with pressure. The window spun open.

While pulling her mask over her mouth, Meeko pointed at her goggles and then out the window. Jet was the first to look. Hypatia could tell by his body language that something out the window surprised him. She also noticed that, like her, he'd grown far leaner and somehow more muscular since they'd come to Regen. He backed away from the window and grabbed Hypatia by the arm, pulling her up to look.

Hypatia squinted against the brightness of the cloudless sky. There were lots of dots against the blue. She forced her nearly closed eyes to open wider and several kites came into focus. Glancing around, she saw that there were actually hundreds of kites. Each one was made from an individual bab leaf. Clumps of them were roughly bouncing on the wind. One clump was very near the ship, but other groupings of anywhere between five and twenty kites were above, below, and off in the distance. Each kite had one leaf attached to a string that held a small scroll at the end of it.

Meeko tapped her on the shoulder to get her attention. She pointed first at Hypatia, then at Jet, and finally down at the floor. She pulled a large metal ring from her coat and took off up the stairs to the door leading to the deck. She opened it, slipped through, and closed it.

The two turned their attention back to the porthole as Meeko fell past. As rapidly as she dropped, she popped back up with lari wings extended. Her lari in full expansion was an amazing sight to behold. Hypatia was jealous. At this range the amount of strength required to control it was obvious, yet Meeko looked like she was born to fly, a bird that had been temporarily grounded on the ship.

It took several bobs and passes to collect the kites, but Meeko managed to grab them all, connecting them to a second tether that disappeared toward the lower levels, out of view of the porthole. Her own line extended upward to the deck. As she collected the last kite, Meeko disconnected the lower tether, closed her lari, and dropped like a stone.

Masterfully, perhaps knowing she had an audience, Meeko soared skyward, coming back into view as she passed the window in a near perfect arc.

A few seconds later she came in the door, breathing hard and full of energy. She flipped closed the window and replaced the handle. Finally pulling down her face mask and raising her goggles in a puff of dust, she said, "Let's go see what the catch of the day is."

They made their way to the lowest level of the Husak, where the large loading doors were. Jet opened the gate and Meeko took hold of the kite-laden tether. The wind tore at them as the two worked in unison to draw the line in. They functioned like the cogs of a clock, and Hypatia's heart was racing at the thought of them together. She couldn't help but imagine Meeko was feeling excited and thinking the same thing. Since Hypatia was never tasked with outside work, she could only cling to a stray pipe and observe with piercing eyes.

Once all the kites were on board, Meeko shut the bay doors.

Hypatia took off her goggles and shook the dust from her hair. *That's another thing,* she thought. *I am sick of the dust.* Iskendar, with all the hardship returning might bring with it, was seeming more and more pleasant with every annoyance on Regen.

All thoughts of Iskendar were wiped with a single word.

"*Arcadia,*" Meeko said.

"What?" Hypatia asked, confused.

"We're in the path of the *Arcadia.*" Meeko was opening several of the rolled notes and stacking the bab leaves. "I should have known. They love these little flyers; they send out hundreds of them."

"Like a message in a bottle." Hypatia was starting to catch her excitement. "On Iskendar, if you were lost at sea, you would send out scrawled messages in an airtight container."

"Yeah, I guess it's the same." Now Meeko looked confused. "Only the Arcadia isn't lost. They send out a bunch of these blythy things thinking they will spread out over a large area. Sometimes, though, if the guy in charge of releasing them does a poor job and screws up, they get stuck up in Arcadia's wake."

Jet was reading some of the scrolls. "They're lists?"

"Yep. Stuff Arcadia needs or wants to trade for." Meeko was proud of being the knowledgeable one, especially when Jet was the one asking questions. "If we know in advance, we can start sorting. Makes transfer quicker and reduces negotiating. We know what they want and we get what we need."

"We're going to meet the Arcadia." Just as she was beginning to process the idea of there being a ship of the Founders nearby, Hypatia was overwhelmed by the idea of seeing it, boarding it. The thought of studying it made her dizzy with excitement.

CHAPTER TWENTY

Today they were meeting up with the Arcadia and Hypatia couldn't contain her excitement. She'd been banished from her regular duties, since her anticipation was manifesting in a ridiculous lack of focus. She'd tied grow wires too loose or too tight, at incorrect angles, and even completely missed two corrections that were critical to the balancing plan. She apologized at length, but even she knew it was best to keep her off important tasks.

Instead of working, Hypatia was standing on the bridge of the Husak and scanning the horizon through the viewport. It was roughly round in shape and, like most of the other parts of the ship, made of used and reused materials. A semi-transparent piece of glass kept the wind at bay. The skies of this world were usually the same shade during daylight hours from edge to edge, so clear windows were unnecessary. Noticing changes, like a flock of blys, an oncoming storm, or an approaching ship was exceptionally easy. It also kept the pilot and captain from having to stare at one endless horizon for weeks. Many of the crew talked about a problem that was specific only to Regen. Meeko called it staring sickness.

"Basically," she had said one long afternoon spent counting piles of bly hides in preparation for trade, "they look at that line for hours and hours and hours, they get tired but don't notice. With eyes open, they drop into sleep. Sometimes no one even catches it until they been like that for who knows how long. Maybe they wake up. Most do."

"But some don't?" Hypatia asked.

"It'll take a few days but either they refresh like waking up from some really dull dream, stretching and all 'what happened?' Or the stare holds on. The body begins to shut down." She said this with little compassion. Death was commonplace on Regen. A fact of life, as short as it usually was. "At some point they stop breathing."

It was a good thing for Hypatia that the glass was semi-transparent, as every particle of focus she had to give was trained on the horizon. She hadn't even blinked for as long as she could recall.

The Arcadia reminded her of home. It reminded her of her Library. She was wrapped up in her own thoughts and questions. *Were there founders of Regen? Does the Arcadia have records? Maybe there is some evidence of Iskendar and Regen sharing a history.*

A dot appeared on the blue sky and it was so small that Hypatia tried to brush it away a few times before realizing what it was. It took all of her willpower to keep from clapping excitedly like a schoolchild. Instead, she allowed herself to blink.

"I see it!" she squeaked as she drew in an eager breath, pointing at the window. She was attempting to indicate the general direction of the dot and looking at the pilot, Meeko's cousin, Current. His friends called him that because he could read the trails of the wind. "Current—I mean sir," she said, forgetting her role on the Husak, "can I go on deck to watch us meet up?"

"Of course. I think I might be able to handle things from here," he said sarcastically. She had been happy to have something, anything, to do. He pulled down a single large lever while cranking a cylindrical column clockwise. "We should be steady enough now. Go. Enjoy." Hypatia smiled and Current smiled back. Trading was an exciting event for those on Regen already but he, and the rest of the crew, couldn't help soaking up some of Hypatia's obvious joy. It was contagious.

She ran down the hallway, grabbing goggles, earplugs, mask, and a safety line.

Bounding up the steps to topside, Hypatia slipped on her safety line and held the end in her other hand. She pushed the heavy door open and the wind rushed down on top of her as she snapped the fasteners of her line to the railing. The railing ran the length of the ship both port and starboard and, in places, over the sides where they might be used when making repairs to the hull of the flying vessel.

Using the safety line, she clipped past three more posts to get the best view of the dot. It had doubled in size since she had last seen it through the bridge viewport, but even twice the size, a dot was still a dot, and she was unable to make out any details.

Hypatia had been standing there for some time when she felt a hand on hers. She grabbed the hand, knowing without looking that it would be Jet.

He pulled on her hand for her attention. She looked over her shoulder and couldn't help thinking how beautiful he looked. His now scraggly hair was being tossed by the wind, the rough whiskers of his untamed beard stuck out below the heavy cloth mask, and the driving wind highlighted his muscular physique, built up with the labour-intensive work. He was beckoning for them to go below.

Turning back to the Arcadia dot, she could tell at this distance that there was no bab tree on it, but that was the only detail she could make out. It was going to be a while before they met up.

Jet and Hypatia made their way, post over post, back to the hatchway.

Once inside the stairwell, Jet helped her down the stairs, recognizing that she was a bit drained. *I do feel a bit tired,* she thought. *And wow, I am so thirsty.* He closed the hatch and started speaking. His lips moved silently and Hypatia was reminded of their first wrighting together. Panic leapt into her mind and she reflexively took his hands to pull him close. Aiming for his mouth, she forgot her mask was still on and planted a dusty, fabric kiss on his lips.

He was still laughing as she removed her earplugs.

"Sorry," she said, feeling her face heat. "I reacted. I forgot about the mask."

He wiped sand from his smiling face, then dusted her down as well. "You've been up there a while. I was starting to think you'd moved in, or out. Or fell off."

"It was just exciting. And so," she paused for effect, "so amazingly *slow.* That dot is just crawling to us."

"Meeko says it will take a long time still, nearly a whole shift. Let's get something to eat."

"And something to drink," she added. "I feel like all the water has been dried up from my body."

They met Meeko in the canteen. "A thing you'll like about the Arcadia," Meeko noted sarcastically, regarding the large glass of water Hypatia was drinking as she sat down, "is that they can filter water and store far more than the Husak."

"Sorry, it was really dry up there," Hypatia said. "And I was out for too long."

"You two drink more water ration than three average Regenites. Should that be Regenettes? Or maybe just Regenner? I'm not used to the idea of Regen being somewhere a person can come from."

"Water is plentiful on Iskendar. We have vast systems for sharing and moving water."

"Don't get her started," Jet added, half joking. "She'll go on about aqueducts and waste water until the babs die."

"Babs die?" Meeko was clearly shocked by this idea. "Babs can't die. They might have bad branches or need to be trimmed at the root, but a bab will always survive." She took a bite of a thin, dry wafer. Her face contorted as she chewed it. "I'll be happy for the trading. I'm sick of these wafers. The Arcadia will have some apples and goat meat."

Hypatia nearly spit out the large gulp of water she had been swallowing. "They have apples and goats? We have those on Iskendar!"

"You have people too," Meeko said. "I think that's enough of a surprise coincidence. Although, doesn't it strike you as a bit odd that we all speak the same language? Worlds away and 'apple' means the same thing? Round red fruit with seeds in the middle of it?"

This was deeper thought than Hypatia had really given to the topic, and she was impressed with Meeko's insight. Though she was not impressed enough to tell her.

Jet jumped in. "On my world we have a few languages. This one is called English, but there's also French."

"English and Latin on Iskendar. Though the second one is mostly just in books or for when people want to show off how smart they are."

"Books. That is the really foreign thing to me," Meeko said. "No time for reading when ya have to work, eat, and sleep." This was more sharing than Meeko had ever done with Hypatia. Jet was her focus. She always had something to tell him or show him. Today, though, she was excited about the trade. Hypatia's infectious anticipation had reached even Meeko.

The entire crew was electric with happy conversation and laughter as well. They had been double- and triple-checking the tradable goods and it was a welcome change of duty from the endless working days. Survival gave way to socializing. The Husak and, as far as Hypatia could tell, all of Regen was a bit brighter.

Meeko rose. "Speaking of rest, I'm off shift so I'm going to catch a nap before the Arcadia gets here." She turned to leave. "Make sure to wake me, Jet." She always singled him out. It rippled Hypatia's skin and irritated her. Meeko smirked, sensing she had achieved her goal. "I don't want to miss it."

Without turning his gaze from Meeko, who was sauntering from the mess hall, Jet said, "She does that to bother you. She knows it gets a rise out of you."

"Oh, I know." Hypatia was watching Jet watch her leave, a fire burning in her chest. She pictured herself holding Meeko over the railing and cutting her safety line with the long blade used for bab trimming. Meeko cried out but the wind drowned out her screams as she slipped away for the ship.

Hypatia and Jet were not allowed on deck as the Husak sidled up to the Arcadia. The timing and expertise required was beyond both their skill levels. Instead they donned their regular topside gear—goggles, mask, hood—and waited eagerly. The usual constant thunder of the wind against the hull was competing with a series of clanging, dragging sounds, and the scraping of wood on metal.

Wordlessly Hypatia stared at the hatch.

"Are you trying to will it open?" Jet asked, his voice coming muffled through his mask.

"Yep," she answered from behind her own thick mask.

As if on cue, the hatch popped open and Meeko stuck her head through. She nodded to Jet and waved them up.

Hypatia bounded up the steps and would have smashed headlong into Meeko if she hadn't reflexively jumped out of the way.

A scored and worn metal wall blocked the normal view of the sky. A portion of the Husak's railing had been moved to create a direct path from the stairs into an open hatchway on the Arcadia. A wooden roof extended from high up on the wall of the Arcadia over the entire hull of the Husak, including the masts, which had their sails collapsed in.

Hypatia turned to the front of the ship and found it difficult to take in just how massive the Arcadia was. She could barely make out the curve of the hull as the length of it slid out of view in the distance. Windowless grey metal continued endlessly into the distance.

Shifting her gaze toward the stern, she saw the same scored grey wall, but it tapered into a rounded cylinder in the distance. Equally as colossal was the height of the Arcadia—it stretched out beyond her line of sight behind the temporary roofing structure.

Glancing back for Jet, she saw Meeko standing provocatively and motioning him to come closer. He looked up at Hypatia, waved, and they continued forward.

They all entered a small vestibule that was only big enough for the three of them. Meeko squeezed past Jet and pulled the outer door closed. The sound of the wind was cut off as the hatch banged shut. It was suddenly weirdly quiet. They had spent months hearing the rumble of the constant gales and having it suddenly absent was strange.

"It's like someone just took one of your senses away," Meeko said, as if reading Hypatia's mind.

"Like I lost something I hadn't even known was there," Jet added.

"Exactly. For those of us not on Arcadia's crew, we never get used to it. In here I feel trapped and tied down. My body can't wait to get back out there."

"How does it do that?" Hypatia asked.

"Ship's airtight." Noticing their questioning looks, Meeko added, "No air in, no air out. Not through the wall, anyways. They have some kind of circulation system in here."

"Okay, how does it fly? It's gigantic." Now over her initial shock, Hypatia's curiosity was taking over.

"Not my area of expertise. A friend told me it has to do with lift and propel. And then some other stuff that's nonsense to me."

"Who is the expert on it?" Hypatia asked, warming to the topic.

"Slow down, Aeych." Jet put his hand on her arm. "First we get aboard, see the sights, and then you can start your interrogation."

"I'm excited." Hypatia shook out her hands. "But I'll play the diplomat, I promise."

"Hey, if you want to know it all, I'll get you Stee. She's an expert on as much as you can be on stuff here." Meeko smiled. "And while ya do that, I'll show Jet around some of the secret and secluded parts of the Arcadia." She wrapped herself around his arm. "The highs, lows, and *everything* in between." Reaching out with her free arm, she pulled another lever and the inner hatchway opened.

The hall on the other side was lit electrically, as was the vestibule they had exited. Hypatia likened the lighting on the Arcadia's smooth walls to the safety lamps that lined the streets of Iskendar. The hallway extended off in different directions that, as Meeko led them into the ship, twisted and turned and seemed to track back on themselves. She walked as if she had memorized the route. "We'll meet up with Stee first. Then get some food," she said over her shoulder.

"What about the Husak and the trades?" Jet asked, worried about his duties, as always. "Should I be helping with that?"

Meeko led them around another turn. "Ye'd be in the way. The Husak'll be docked for days. Unloading, loading, and repairs is captain stuff. Dad'll have it sorted."

They turned down yet another corridor, their boots clanking on the metal grating of the floor. "How big is the ship?" Hypatia asked.

"Hmm, I've never thought of it. I'd say up and down there are nearly thirty floors. Port to starboard, twice that size. Front to back, four times that. Biggest ship in the fleet and this next room is the biggest part of 'er."

They passed through a doorway onto a metal landing that overlooked a cavernous room with vaulting ceilings. The distance down from the landing was the height of the Great Library, as was the distance up to the ceiling from the landing. The room could easily completely house two large buildings from Iskendar. People were walking about in front of a giant machine along the back of one wall. The machine was made of the same grey metal as the hull and was so large, it met both the floor and ceiling, with the base wider near the floor. At the centre of the base was a fogged glass window from which a bright, nearly white flame was emanating. The light of the flame pulsed along glowing lines that extended out in all directions along the body of the machine. The angular lines never intersected and appeared to carry the light out of the room through the floor and ceiling. Hypatia guessed the people moving about in front of the machine were keeping it working or reading output from it.

At the other end of the room, more people were moving about. Some were sitting and eating while others appeared to be lined up, waiting to be served. Several groups were just standing around, probably socializing.

Meeko saw something that made her smile and run down the stairs. "Stee!" she called.

A woman sitting at one of the tables in the distance looked up. "Meeko!" She popped up from the table and strode quickly toward the stairs.

Jet and Hypatia hung back on the stairs, taking in the massiveness of the room and watching Meeko running toward her friend.

Before they could reach each other the space around them appeared to seize, as if it was frozen. All the bustle and movement at both ends of the room ceased. Everything hung for only a few moments until, as if frame by frame, the world began filling in the pieces. With each frame a black shape was forming in mid-air in the centre of the room. It started as a hollow and nearly indescribable form. As the moments moved forward the shape became a beastly skull.

Frames continued clicking by, each change adding another piece to the shape. The process was gaining speed. A neck came next. A sinew of darkness followed and stretched from the head, pulling tight on shoulders as broad as the machine. The shape was still thirty feet above the floor, assembling downward faster and faster. Chest. Arms. Waist.

Then came the claws.

CHAPTER TWENTY-ONE

"It has blades for arms," Hypatia said, awestruck.

"I see it," Jet replied.

Hypatia recognized the long, curved blades as scythes. They were so large that no person would have been able to wield them. They replaced the beast's forearms, the blades emerging from its elbows, the tips resting on the deck. The legs were forming now—muscular thighs and hocks and the cloven hooves of a goat for feet.

When the beast was fully formed, the frames stopped and everything went still. The air shifted and Hypatia heard Jet inhale before he shouted, "Run! Now!"

Screams broke out below.

Hypatia backed away as the shadowy hulk of the monster began to move. The outline of the beast's torso rose and fell, as if the monster was breathing heavily.

"I said run!"

She turned to look at Jet, who passed her and pounded down the stairs, drawing his canne from somewhere in his clothes as he ran. The grating of the stairs was open enough that she could see him several flights down as he vaulted over the railing and landed in a crouch, poised to pounce.

The beast was crouching as well. When it leapt she felt it before she saw it moving.

The stairs shuddered and the blackness filled the room above them. The monster came down with tremendous force, leading with the scythe of its right arm. The blade cleaved a table and the woman seated there in half. Scraping metal screamed loud enough that Hypatia had to cover her ears.

Jet leapt into view before her and landed beside the beast. He was circling, trying to get behind it. Holding the sticks low as he ran, he kept his gaze locked on his prey.

Sensing Jet was there, the monster turned, swinging the other arm out low. Jet jumped clear of it. The beast's momentum drove the scythe into the side of the ship. It tore metal.

Jet was behind it and jumped onto its back. He dropped out of Hypatia's sight.

Ripping its arms free from the wall and the floor, the monster tried to spin. As it did, Jet came into view. The monster sliced toward a group cowering in the corner near the glowing machine. They had nowhere to run. The scythe tore through their bodies. Screams rang throughout the cavernous room. The monster brought its other arm around for another blow. Metal ripped and the blade disappeared below the level of the floor.

Jet was on its head, grasping a handful of darkness and swinging across the back of it, raining blows on its skull with his canne as he moved. The monster screeched and drew a bloody arm from the floor.

The wind howled into the room and the pressure changed. The monster had breached the hull.

In response, the Arcadia tilted and began a spin. It halted at about a tenth of a turn, enough to knock the mountainous beast sideways and off balance. Jet tumbled to the floor. He rolled and recovered quickly, popping up to his feet, but one of the monster's flailing legs pinned him.

Hypatia ran down the steps to the next landing.

The beast was trying to prop itself up enough to stand, but it couldn't leverage itself up. Jet screamed in pain as the leg crushed him into the wall.

Hypatia was at floor level now, dashing toward him.

Dropping from out of nowhere, a screaming Meeko used her downward force to drive a broken pipe into the pinning leg. Reacting to the pain, the monster yanked the massive foot back. Jet slid down from the wall and Meeko dragged him out of the way. She followed it up by jumping back onto the monster, stabbing at it with her hands. Hypatia could see some kind of metal spike protruding from each fist. She dodged an upward swing from the arm, but it connected with the wall and tore through it. Sunshine poured in along with more rushing wind as the beast slid out the gash in the hull.

"Meeko!" Hypatia cried as Meeko dropped from view.

The Arcadia spun and for brief moment Hypatia could see both the monster and the girl who had been her enemy dropping toward the ground below. Her heart tore in two.

Then she slid toward the same gash.

Hypatia threw her hands out, searching the floor for anything to grasp but finding only smooth polished floor. Hypatia slid through the opening.

Someone grabbed her as the wind hit her.

She was still falling, but now she was no longer falling alone. Jet was pulling her toward him as they tumbled downward. She threw her arms around him.

Looking past Jet, she glimpsed the Arcadia as they spun away from it. Engulfed in smoke and fire, it slowly sank from the sky. It had pitched forward enough that Hypatia knew there was no hope for them. Thinking of Chezpa, the crew of the Husak, and even Meeko all going to ground, she was more afraid for them in that moment than herself.

The reality of their own situation was hard to ignore. They had stopped spinning but they were falling with terminal velocity.

Jet whispered in her ear and Regen faded.

CHAPTER TWENTY-TWO

They crashed gasping to the floor of the Great Library in the dead of night.

She was on her feet at once. "What have we done, Jet?"

"You didn't cause this."

"No Jet, I didn't. *We* did." She was clenching her fists, still staring at the floor. "I've dreamt about those things, the monsters. They came from me. But you . . ." She trailed off, too angry, too hurt to finish the statement.

"I? I what?"

If she opened her mouth now, Hypatia knew that the words she spoke would be devastating to Jet. Full of blame and anger and rage.

"How can this be our fault, Aeych? This is the enemy we have been at war with. Centuries old. My home was destroyed by them."

"We brought them there. If you hadn't taught me about wrighting then we couldn't have poisoned Regen. She is dead, Jet. Meeko is dead because of us. All those people are dead."

"You don't know that. Maybe she got away."

"They went to ground, Jet! On Regen ground is death to them. There were no other ships nearby, not even a spire to cling to—nothing."

"To blame yourself is a waste of time. Sooner or later the Kek would have—"

"The what?" She was livid.

"The Kek. I was saved by people who were wrighting before they knew how on my world. The Kek were there before them. The Kek were on my adopted world, as well. They appear sooner or later."

"You know what they are called? You knew they could appear at any moment? You didn't tell me?"

Jet was silent. He looked away.

"Tell me, Jet. Tell me. I deserve to know."

"I am sorry, Aeych." He sounded ashamed. "We were happy. It was a life I always dreamed of. You and I are meant to be together. But I let a dream of us put everything and everyone at risk. Just being in a place without Kek—you can't understand how it feels to be so . . ." he paused, searching for the right word " . . . safe."

"So Regen was some kind of Elysium for you, was it?" Another point suddenly struck Hypatia. "And so was Iskendar! You put my home in harm's way so you could feel safe?"

"I came to your world to save it. That's why we wright. Sometimes the Kek are too powerful, impossible to stop—or they already won."

"But Regen had none of the—" she paused to spit out the word; even the thought of it left a sour taste "—Kek."

"I know. Something caused them to appear."

"Us Jet, it was us. Or me. Something is tearing at me, something dark."

"I don't want to believe that, but I have no other explanation."

Hypatia shuddered. "Iskendar is in trouble now too."

"It isn't. We can stop them if they appear."

"Tell that to Meeko. Tell that to her father. Tell that to everyone on that ship." Tears were welling in her eyes as the impact of what had happened and what needed to happen started to settle in. "She said there was a thousand people on the Arcadia—farmers, miners, traders, families, children. All of them are dead. How safe can my home be when, in one swoop, we destroy the lives a thousand innocent people?"

The Library felt cold and dark. It had been a refuge, a blanket, to Hypatia, even in the darkest nights of study or when she was fighting with the Librarian, the mayor, or her mother. It was her own sanctuary. Now the endless aisles and dark corners were portals, the darkness waiting to vomit forth hordes of the Kek. Hypatia pictured them in her mind streaming from the Library, claws at the ready, teeth gnashing and red eyes piercing her soul.

"You have to leave, Jet." She said this with the conviction of The Catalogue of Iskendar.

"I can't leave you," he replied reflexively, as if it was instinct.

"If you leave now," she continued in the same cold tone, "maybe my home has a chance."

"Aeych, you can't wish me gone like this," he pleaded.

"Everyone was right about you, Jet." Hypatia knew this part was going to hurt, but she kept the hollow tone. "You are dangerous, foreign, and a hazard to the philosophy of the Founders of Iskendar."

He grabbed her by the shoulders and lifted her from the floor. It wasn't

106

forceful and she let herself be lifted by him. "I'm not dangerous. I wright to help." He was staring right into her. His dark blue eyes were reaching out to her, begging that he be heard and understood. "I do it to fight."

"There isn't anything here to fight, Jet!" The Catalogue was cracking under the pressure of his intensity. She pushed him back and he pulled her in tighter. He opened his mouth to speak again but she cut him off. "You stay long enough, and maybe there will be something to fight. Monsters, terrible evil things in my home, because of us. So we can be together, Iskendar gets suffering, horror, and death. Won't that be beautiful?"

"Aeych, you are being unreasonable."

She pulled away from him successfully this time. "Then Iskendar can be just like your home. Your world."

"That's not fair. I was a child."

"So was Meeko. So are thousands on Regen and millions on Iskendar. Will you save them, Jet? All I see is glass, silence, and darkness at the end. Like the world you first showed me. Beautiful, silent. Dead."

"We will fight it."

"I said it already, Jet. There is nothing to fight here. No reason for you to come to Iskendar. You wright to help. Well Jet, you can't help. Leave."

"Aeych, I have a reason."

He kept using her nickname and that was beginning to annoy her because she kept thinking of her mother. It was twisting her thoughts to all the ways her mother could die because of them. "I don't want to hear it." She knew what he was going to say and that she was going to be unable to stop him from saying it.

"I wright for you." He paused to see if it hit her. He was hoping that some final heartfelt plea of his love would save it and give them some chance. "You are the only reason the universe is worth wrighting for."

Hypatia was fighting back tears. "I'm not worth it. We aren't worth the lives of a billion people."

"You are."

"Leave." The tears were flowing now in defiance of her attempt to sound cold and detached.

"I can't."

"My world, my family, my life are everything to me. You . . ." She hesitated because the next part was going to hit him harder than going to ground on Regen. "You are a stranger."

"Aeych—"

"Don't call me that. Leave. *Never* come back."

"Aeych, please." He reached for her and she slapped his hand away.

"Don't call me that, stranger," she spat. "Leave!"

"I can't imagine my world without you."

"And my world will be as dead as yours if you stay. Do you want that, stranger? Get lost. The longer you stand here, the more of a stranger you become. Every moment gives me another chance to realize how foreign you really are. Now leave."

"Aeych, it's me, Jet."

"Do not use that name *ever* again. Stranger." Each time she said it she could sense him breaking. "Leave and do not ever set a foot on Iskendar again!" She shoved him hard in the chest.

He pulled the book from his side and flipped it open to the page he wanted with a flick of the wrist and not a single thought.

Looking down at the book, he whispered.

"Don't *ever* come back!"

As the words from the book slipped from his mouth, Hypatia covered her ears and closed her eyes. The crashing finale of the gatewright confirmed he was gone and she crumpled to the floor. Hypatia grabbed her face and began loudly sobbing. She was now processing the shock of the destruction on Regen, of losing Meeko and, mostly, from banishing Jet from her world.

Just as she was there when Hypatia wrighted back the first time, Kalli was waiting in the dark. She stepped forward and spoke.

"Get up."

Hypatia gasped for breath and tried to stand.

"Stop your pointless weeping and stand up," Kalli demanded.

Pulling herself together, Hypatia stood.

"Your clothes are a disgrace and the rest of your appearance is not worthy of any discussion. You will go home. Greet your family warmly. Then bathe. Do you understand?"

Hypatia nodded and moved to leave.

"I am not done with your direction yet. Once you have rested and eaten, you will return to the Library to work. You will assume the position you were assigned as if no time has passed."

"Will the people wonder where I have been?"

"I did not request your questions. You will accept what I have said. I do not expect to see you until tomorrow." Kalli stared her down.

"I understand," Hypatia softly replied.

"Now leave. Try not to be seen in your current state."

Hypatia hurried home, her anxiety and shame compounded by sorrow at the loss of so many. "So many died on Regen that no one on Iskendar will ever know," she said to herself.

She stumbled through the door and into her bedroom. Too exhausted to change or bathe, she climbed into her bed and closed her eyes.

She woke at the sound of her mother's voice.

"What happened here, Quint? There is a mess from the front door all over the foyer, like you dragged in dirt. And it even goes upstairs." Her mother's voice was getting louder. Aurelia was headed for Hypatia's room. She was following the trail of dirt. "Why didn't you clean this up, Quint?"

Hypatia sat up and tried to make herself look presentable. Her mother glanced into her room as she was walking by, then stopped dead, gaping.

"Mom?" Hypatia asked sheepishly.

"Aeych? Oh for goodness—are you really here?"

"I am. I'm so sorry I…"

Before she could finish the sentence, Aurelia had her arms wrapped tight around her, squeezing the breath from her lungs. "Your father said you would never come home. The note. We thought you were lost. I told him." She said all this as she rocked Hypatia within her bear hug, Then she started peppering kisses all over her face. "He will be so happy you are home."

"He won't be mad?"

"Oh, he will be mad and you will be punished severely, if you aren't too old for us to do that. But he will cry with joy at seeing his baby come home. Now shower, dress, and come down. My goodness, you need to eat."

Hypatia looked forward to the promised meal as she bathed and dressed.

Quint shed several tears when he saw Hypatia walk into the kitchen. Aurelia had told him of her return and had to physically restrain him from rushing in to greet her as she was dressing, her mother told Hypatia. "'Privacy be forgotten. I need to see my child,' he said," she quoted Quint with a joyful laugh.

Instead she had sat him down at the table and made him a coffee. He was sipping it as Hypatia entered. He set the coffee down and swiped the moisture from his reddened eyes before rising to envelop her in his arms.

The three of them settled into a light breakfast and Hypatia ate more than her share. Her father remarked how thin she now seemed and her mother had encouraged her to take as much as she wanted. They determined that she was too old for punishment from her parents but lamented how the papers had dragged her name through the mud when she disappeared.

"I hope it didn't hurt your reputation when I went," Hypatia said. "I never meant for that disgrace on my family. It was my decision alone."

"Your mother and I are sturdier stock than that. We will recover. As long as Jet is gone, I am sure we can rebuild from here on."

She felt The Catalogue take over. "He is a stranger to me now. I believe we will not see him again."

Her parents didn't ask her what happened or where she had been. Hypatia believed it was better that way. For all the excitement and newness she had experienced, there was so much darkness she wanted to push down and forget.

CHAPTER TWENTY-THREE

Hypatia returned to the Library that night after spending the day in her home with her parents. All that was familiar, and now foreign, as well. She had no desire to contact friends or acquaintances. When evening came she simply collected her things and left for the Library, grateful for the shadows of sunset. This repeated for weeks, and Aurelia saw no improvement in her outlook.

Aurelia, wanting to have her confident and joyful daughter back, reached out to Gaius.

"I still picture myself beside her." Gaius's eyes were trained on the ground and he was shuffling his feet like a child, sweeping the dirt from the cobblestones into the cracks as if it were a dry mortar. "But now I imagine her with a far-off look in her eyes. No smile on her face."

He was holding two tickets to the theatre that Aurelia had purchased for herself and her daughter. The plan, as she explained it, was for Gaius to meet Hypatia there instead.

"You can still have happiness with her," she said, knowing he was eager but sensing he was also defensive.

"I could be happy. With Hypatia I could always feel my place, my home, my heart." He glanced up at Aurelia. "But it wouldn't be enough. As much as I want it, I want her happiness more than my own. That is all I will ever be satisfied with."

Gaius had struggled when Hypatia had disappeared. He made few appearances at the coffee shop and even when he was seen there, he did not engage in his normal banter. The jovial tone Gaius was known for was gone.

"You would give up fighting for her? How can you be idle when he steals in and tries to whisk her away? I know you. Your whole life, you have looked upon her with the universe in your eyes." On cue, he looked down again. Aurelia resumed with renewed vigour. "Why aren't you putting up a fight?"

Gaius looked surprised by her ferocity and shot back with equal ferocity, "You think I want to give her up? My heart is shattered. You tell me what to do. Even now, with Jet supposedly gone for good, you can't change someone's heart. Believe me, if I could change my own, I would."

"You could try." She reached over and took his hand, softening her tone. "She values you as a friend. If you don't give up, she will retreat into your arms. Once the passion of waiting for him—counting the long days since she saw him last, the hours and minutes—wears her down, she will realize you are always there. For her."

He still looked at the ground wordlessly. Aurelia rose from her seat and crouched before him, forcing him to meet her gaze. "Get in there. Show her *you*, Gaius: world-renowned coffee baron, king of social circles, keeper of secrets, friend of the Assistant to the Great Librarian—show her you are always there. Show her she will never have to wonder when you might come back."

"I can't be her plan B."

Aurelia sighed and stood. "You deserve to be happy. She loved you before he came. The love is still there, all you need do is remind her." She sat in silence for an awkward amount of time, waiting for a response or any reaction.

"I do," he whispered, and slowly looked up at Aurelia. The tears were pooling in his eyes, then slipping down his cheeks as he blinked them away. "I do want her." He withdrew a handkerchief from his jacket pocket. The cloth was clearly well worn and badly in need of a wash.

She hugged him as she would her own son. She imagined, in that hug, what it would be like if one day he was.

CHAPTER TWENTY-FOUR

Hypatia could hear a voice mumbling, off in the distance. From some corner it spoke when she thought of wright paths, and when the words triggered a pattern in her mind. When she thought of Jet the voice was there too, mumbling indistinguishable words. At first she assumed it was guilt manifested from all that was lost on Regen, the cries of hundreds echoing in their destruction.

A rumbling murmur always persisted in her mind when it was quiet. It was quiet a lot during the night shift in the Library, when the patrons were few and too busy to speak. The voice was deep. It wasn't sinister outright, but it was cold. It was patient. There was no hurry in the chanting. There was no reaching and no calling out to her. It hovered at the edge of her mind.

Connecting patterns was easier with the voice. It would take her hand as she strode down the aisles, streets, and forests of her mental catalogue. She could feel the voice directing, supporting, and encouraging patiently.

A calm, infinite patience.

It was humming this night. Or maybe it purred. Hypatia found it difficult to tell, but she felt reassured by it and it, in turn, had been getting more involved with her current attempt to find a gateway to wright.

The trigger had been a passage: *shape, shift and trick the past* and as she read it Geb—*where had she heard that name before?*—had asserted himself. A low rumbling that warmed into a familiar purring pulsed in Hypatia's temples and radiated through her being.

She tucked herself into the historical resources on the first floor, a manual open in front of her.

My girl, Geb said calmly.

Hypatia, without hesitation, answered in her head, Yes?

I like your mind. It was still purring as it spoke. So vast. The words are endless.

She felt her hands closing the book in front of her.

I can guide you.

"I know. I feel you pull me." She raised the book but hesitated to put it away. Looking down the aisle, she could see that it extended into a dark forest, the books and the Library gone. But there was something else familiar in the woods.

Think of me as your accompanist. You play the lead, I support.

"That sounds more ordered than you like it."

Ah, the voice sighed happily, *but you play off the page. The story, fate, it ends the same. The path and the tale that follows a familiar structure . . . but you make the piece your own.*

"What if I fight you? You can't help direct me if I'm not willing to play your song ." The trees in the forest shivered and cracked. Brown leaves were falling and turning to dust before they reached the carpet of the Library.

That is the joy of being the accompanist. I find your melody. I guide you when you get lost and I lift your sound to another level. I make you fly. I make you better. I make you whole. Fighting me only makes it more chaotic, more fun and . . .

Was the voice laughing?

. . . much, much messier.

She knew this was a threat. The voice wanted her to fight and wanted the mess. The cost of life, of sanity, would be higher and the fault for it would lie squarely at her feet. The smell of rot pervaded the forest, which was encircling her. Fate had a melody she was bound to play. It would be her song, but there was no escaping the outcome.

"Where does it end?"

There is no end. Only chaos. Cyclical. Infinite. Chaos. Music is the perfect beauty in the noise. Music is the harmonic cacophony of the universe. From the beginning to the end of time.

The voice growled a long, low sound before continuing.

Do you want to know? I can give you that.

"Know? Know what?"

"Everything." The voice came from behind her.

She dropped the book as she felt a hand slip behind her waist. The volume bounced off the shelf and fell to the floor. The sound echoed loudly in the Library. A chair squeaked as it was pushed back from an unseen table.

The noise startled Hypatia and she bent to pick up the dropped book. As she rose, a black void, full of gaping mouths and with thousands of white teeth, smiled at her from the end of the aisle. A single eye opened in the centre of the mass.

Inside her head the growl rumbled to a clamour and the void launched at her. She screamed and fell back.

It dissolved as it reached her, turning into the face of a young politico who looked terrified at her reaction.

"I'm sorry," he yelped. "I was just trying to see if there was a problem."

Hypatia inhaled quickly, trying in vain to recover. "No, it was my fault." The man held a hand out to help her up and she reached up to take it.

I can guide you.

She yanked her hand back in revulsion. "What?"

"I said I can help you up, but . . ." He was very unsure of what was going on, any intention of being chivalrous wiped from his face. Glancing around to see if he was missing something, he added, "I could go, if you prefer."

"No, no." She waved a hand toward him, trying to look recovered. "I'll go. I need a break anyway." Hypatia scrambled to her feet and hurried away.

As she left the building she noticed the sun was shining, and wondered where the night had gone. Once she had put some distance between herself and the Library, she stood looking out from the Capital's core. She had a clear view of her quiet neighbourhood. Floating above those homes was an expansive blue sky. It blocked her view of the stars. Jet was there. Somewhere past the blue. Perhaps she might be looking in the wrong direction, but she hoped he felt her fear. She hoped something sparked in him and made him come running.

The clanging of a bell startled Hypatia from her reverie. That was a call to the amphitheatre, and she recalled the show her mother had invited her to. It wiped away the distractions and fear and Geb as she realized she was late for the theatre. *Did I lose a whole night and day?* she thought. The bell tolled again, telling her she could make it in time with a quick sprint.

Slowing as she got close to the amphitheatre, Hypatia saw Gaius chatting with two beautiful women. She recognized them both—one was a brilliant mathematician and the other, Telesilla by name, was head of the progressive initiative committee. She chose those ideas that would see debate and ultimately could decide the flow of technological advancement in the Capital. Those changes would echo throughout Iskendar.

They both seemed to be urging him into the amphitheatre and Gaius was resisting. As Hypatia got close, she could hear him thanking the women for their concern.

"I'll be fine. I'm sure my company will be along." He noticed Hypatia approach. "Ah, here she is now."

"Gaius, it is wonderful to see you here." Hypatia smiled at him, genuinely pleased to be in his company. She felt warmer suddenly.

Telesilla coughed low and Hypatia wondered if she was indicating some displeasure with her presence. "Greetings, Assistant. I do hope you and Gaius enjoy the evening."

Hypatia looked at Gaius and immediately understood. Knowing the importance of appearances, she played along without question. "On such a beautiful night with such attractive company," she looked toward Gaius, still smiling, "I am sure I will."

The ladies moved quickly away, turning to whisper something to each other as they did. Telesilla was intentionally loud enough for Hypatia to hear her say that Gaius would likely be as abandoned as her Library.

"I am sorry for the ruse." Gaius waved the tickets from her mother. "I appreciate that you played along."

"No ruse would have been required." She mentally thanked her mother; a night with Gaius and his light conversation would be better than the endless lecture of a parent. "We are friends. I would always say yes to an invitation from you." She could see him physically lighten and she took his arm to urge him along.

"That makes me very happy," Gaius said, handing his tickets to the usher. "Your mother has been worried and I know—"

"Let's not talk about my mother."

"I will stroke the name from the conversation topic list."

"Also, if we could leave any worry about my personal state at the door." Hypatia saw several groups notice the two enter and start gossiping in tightly closed circles. "Though I am guessing that might be hard to escape," she added.

"Keep your eyes on the performers or upon me. That way you can only see beauty. As when I look upon you."

She laughed. "Always so forward." Despite her response, she took the opportunity to look him over. The last few months had aged him heavily. Stress had wrought new lines on his face and he appeared thinner. His eyes had lost some of their shine. She blushed, realizing they were glowing still because he was looking at her. *Perhaps Gaius*, she thought. *Perhaps you and I.*

They were pulled from the moment by a call from the stage to find their seats. They shyly looked away from each other and Gaius led them into the main amphitheatre and down the stairs.

Eyes turned and Hypatia did what she could to ignore the angry and brooding faces that gazed up at her. They continued down twenty rows of stone steps to the orchestra.

"Front row; it should make for a nice view," Gaius remarked, attempting to distract his date.

Even as they sat down, she could feel the glares boring into the back of her head. Snippets of "Can you believe" and "She really is back in public after that" and "How could she ever?" drifted down on them.

Gaius spoke loudly, feeling Hypatia's tension. "I hear the company has reworked the piece unexpectedly."

Reflexively Hypatia commented, "They always do, don't they?" She thought that might have sounded colder than she'd intended and added, "I look forward to their reinvention."

"I've taken steps to have your favourite coffee delivered at intermission."

"It isn't like you to remove the element of surprise, Gaius."

"I want to give you something to look forward to."

"Being with you is enough for that. I am unnerved by the attention we are getting, but your company is warming and friendly. The brightness you shine upon me lightens all shadows they might cast."

He took her hand and squeezed. Gaius opened his mouth to say something, but a masked actor had taken the stage and was speaking before he could get any words out.

"The king comes this very night to our sacred place." The clay mask's features were exaggerated, with huge eyes and a mouth to match. "Take heed, our queen does not leave trace." The voice, disconcerting to Hypatia, sounded hollow as it escaped from the frozen face of the mask. "It is Oberon occupied of anger and equipped of wrath," the lithe actor bounced from the orchestra up to the proscenium, "For Titania, taken a child he, himself would have,"

Hypatia was drawn in to actor's movements as much as the words. He seemed to light upon the stage without touching down at all. The impish expression captured on the mask extended to the very core of the delivery and movement. The script echoed outward from the gaping mouth, rising from a deep well and resonating inside her mind.

> *And now they meet in groves once green,*
> *Where charred, dead fountains ne'r run clean.*
> *Finale of all to fear and dark to blight,*
> *A pair creep to death not once, but twice will wright.*

"These words are changed." Hypatia looked to see how Gaius would be reacting. He knew this play as well as she did and would be shocked at the twisted revision they'd made. His face was frozen in the same expression as the fairy who spoke before them.

"Gaius?" Hypatia whipped her gaze back to the stage only to be a foot away from the clay mask, yawning wide in front of her. She screamed.

The mask bared teeth and closed the remaining distance to her, the mouth crashing shut at the tip of her nose. She flinched away from it reflexively, feeling the moist heat of breath on her face. She shook in fear. It spoke in guttural tones, almost an animal growl. The words rattled her skull.

A merrier hour was never wasted there.
So make space my friends, as the king appears.

Gaius was shaking her lightly. "Hypatia?" he sounded concerned and distant. In her mind she moved toward him and found herself slipping out from a laced shroud. The darkness was lifting from something.

She blinked and became immediately aware that hundreds of eyes were upon her and that everyone present, audience and actors alike, had gone silent.

"Excuse us!" Gaius said loudly and ushered her toward the steps. Hypatia was surprised to find she had already been standing. She took laboured steps toward the exit. "Please continue." He waved a hand and the actor, completely out of character by this point, took a moment to remember what he was doing.

He cleared his throat, jumped onstage, and continued.

Hypatia put a hand to her chest as they cleared the inner theatre area. "I am so sorry. I—"

Gaius cut her off. "There is nothing to be sorry for. Let's get out of here."

She attempted to apologize again but Gaius turned away and led them into the street. They walked on silently. Hypatia could feel Gaius had his back up. There was no anger, but his stress was high enough that she thought she could smell it.

He started to speak when they were beyond the lights of the building. ""None of us, not I, nor your mother, know what you have been through. You should not expect anyone to understand your stress and so, your actions. No apologies are required."

"Screaming in a theatre is worth apologizing for."

"You did not scream, Hypatia."

She was sure that the scream was hers. In the moment the mask expanded . . .

"You stood and shouted at the top of your lungs."

"What did I say?"

Gaius looked nervous.

"Tell me."

"You announced loudly the coming of the king, and about death." He said it quickly and Hypatia guessed he was hiding more.

"That makes no sense. Why would I?"

"And you almost bit down on Telesilla's nose. She and the other woman had been sitting behind us. She screamed at you and suddenly you backed off."

Hypatia was trying to picture herself in the place of the clay mask. Staring out at Telesilla, baring her teeth and lunging at her. "Well that does warrant an apology," she said after a moment. "And how embarrassed you must be. I am sorry for that."

"It was worth the trouble. Don't mind my feelings." He smiled impishly and she was reminded of the actor. "They deserved it for their rudeness. Let's get you home. I think rest would be the best solution. The Librarian has you working too hard, I suspect."

"She has, not to mention she has added lectures for me to give at the college. None of it justifies my behaviour, though."

Gaius pulled her arm under the crook of his and began walking. She allowed him to lead. "The strangeness you must have experienced, what happened to you in those weeks you were gone . . . those who don't know are in no place to judge you or the things you do."

"I know you mean well, but they are. Iskendar has rules and I am to be held to the highest account. What I did tarnishes me, my family, and now you."

"I sell coffee, Hypatia. My reputation is only as good as the addictions I support. And they are hooked. No action of yours could change that."

Despite his protest, Hypatia was aware that the shop had been on the downturn recently, largely due to Gaius spending time away. He was as much the business as the beverages he served. Knowing he meant well, she kept the information to herself.

Gaius spoke again after a minute of silence. "You know I am here for you, Hypatia."

"I do. I am thankful for that."

"If you plan to be here I will support you, no judgment, no apologies required."

"That is the most I can ask of any friend, Gaius."

"As more than a friend, as well."

She'd known this was coming and sought to avoid it. Her heart belonged to Jet and she was unable to picture a time when it could be anyone else. She wanted to keep Gaius close, but it hurt to know he would be waiting for her unlikely commitment. "You deserve more."

"I will wait."

"I know you will, and I am torn apart knowing that you could miss out on love and happiness because of my . . . ." She didn't know what to call her love for Jet. He was gone, likely forever. Would this be her mourning? She

119

had to wonder.

"It is my choice to make. There is no woman on Iskendar that can keep my eye, my mind, and my heart as you do."

"Take me home please, Gaius. Tonight was stressful enough. Worrying about your mistakenly placed love and my arrogance is more than we should bear on such an occasion."

"I will do as you desire."

"Talk to me about coffee," she said, pulling him close while trying to judge the right amount of distance she should keep between friends and nothing more.

"That," he said, "I can do."

He told her about rare blends and isolated coffee growers from around Iskendar, highlighting those he had only recently been able to procure through patience and great care.

CHAPTER TWENTY-FIVE

It was during an assigned lecture to a group of third year historical majors that Hypatia had "volunteered" to give that she received the news of the tragedy in the south.

A murmur gathered at the back of the room as voices in the hall outside the lecture room drifted in. Hypatia could make out a few words and she slowed what she had been dictating. The chatter leapt rapidly between the previously attentive students.

" . . . from the cliffs . . ."

" . . . called to their doom . . ."

" . . . suicides by the hundreds . . ."

" . . . like stunned sheep . . ."

" . . . Medini."

She raised a hand and a hush slowly fell over the students, many of whom now appeared shaken and distracted. "Who knows the details?" Hypatia asked, mostly directing the request toward the rear of the room, where a few wanderers from the hall had come in to share the news. "And if you can avoid hearsay or rumour, I think that would be best."

A young man who had been standing in the doorway spoke. "I received the news directly from the official courier for Medini. It is as close to true as can be expected, this far from the south."

"Come up here then, and share what you know."

Unmoving, he said, "It is rather disturbing and I am afraid some gathered here might—"

She knew where he was going with this and had no patience for it. "They will find out now, or soon enough."

"Right. Yes. Of course," he stammered, and descended the steps. He half turned at the bottom of the lecture hall to address Hypatia and the students simultaneously. "The official news from Medini is reporting tragedy. Not war or natural disaster, but supernatural in nature."

"I requested you not allude to rumour, and supernatural causes do slip into that territory." She fought to suppress the images of the beast on Regen as she said this.

"It is not rumour," the young man replied, attempting to appear humbled. "It was witnessed by more than half of the survivors in the city."

"Survivors?" The image of the Arcadia split open and Meeko falling through the sky leapt into Hypatia's mind.

"Near suppertime, voices were heard at the edges of the city. The quiet of such a late hour allowed sounds to carry throughout Medini. But the voices did not belong to the townsfolk. Hundreds of people were, um . . ." He struggled for the right word " . . . they were entranced in mere moments. Not all who heard the voices were struck; the numbers indicate one in four were taken."

"Taken?" As Hypatia asked she heard the same word pass between the students in shock and curiosity.

"Lured might be more apt. Those entranced got up from their meals or conversations and made directly for the cliffs."

"Did anyone try to stop them?" a girl asked, clearly shaken.

"They did, but the victims reacted violently to any restraint. There was fierce fighting and early reports of deaths in the streets and in homes. The worst came, however, to those who made it to the cliffs. With serene confidence and pleasure on their faces, the victims flung themselves to the rocky waters below." The room was silent now. The man continued after a brief pause. "Many were heard talking of little people or 'wisps' of immeasurable beauty."

"What of the government of the city?" Hypatia asked, thinking specifically of Mamercus.

"A good many of those in the diplomatic and ruling body of Medini perished. There has been no account of the names yet. This is only the first word. I am told more details will come as the emissaries arrive in the Capital. They are en route to request assistance."

"And they shall receive it. Is there to be a meeting?"

"Yes, but I do not know the details."

"Are there any more to tell? Details, I mean."

"Only the numbers. Nearly a quarter of the city population lost, and the casualties are highest amongst children and the elderly."

"The news is truly dreadful, but let us be thankful it was not all the people of the great city of Medini." The Catalogue had taken over and she let the confidence and apathy slide in—she could not bear the weight of this grief. "Class," she addressed the room, "we shall dismiss under such news. I expect any further concentration on study to be impossible."

As the class shuffled out, loudly chattering, Hypatia turned her attention to putting books away and generally cleaning up following the lesson. She was wiping the board when the low hum began to vibrate in the corner of her mind.

It was as if a shape was sliding into her consciousness. She was looking at the blackboard as the classroom twisted before her. A sloping curve of smooth black stone became a familiar road with a familiar voice. The weight of the thing on the road before her was so great that the ground hummed in vibration as it approached. Her hands brushed away the remaining words on the blackboard and she saw the shadowed thing dragging forward on its surface. It disturbed the chalk dust as it drew near, creating hints of its size and shape. The world between her globe and reality drew closer together.

A worm pushed out of the board, sloughing off white powder as it did. It spoke without moving in a voice she knew well. "Did you like that, Hypatia?"

"It was you?"

"Of me. Yes." It stopped and Hypatia thought it might be taking a breath. "The chaos works through fear. I do not choose the manifestation. Only fear." The monster paused again and she could hear it sigh warmly. "Your mind cradles the fear and births the darkness it finds there."

"Why?"

"There is no why. It is. It will." The voice inside her head was enjoying this. There was a smile in the tone it used. "At the end of all things, at the beginning, there is chaos."

"Iskendar is doomed, then." Hypatia felt defeated.

"It is. It was inevitable."

"I need Jet. He can fight this." She turned defiantly toward it in her mind and in the classroom.

The voice laughed. It was loud but she could not block it out, as it came from within. She thought she might be laughing too. It blocked out her thoughts and drowned her focus.

"You are so precious. I am the darkest and lightest corners of your mind. A person does not suffer chaos and come out whole. Your world will fall again. Iskendar will fall, again."

The words echoed in her head.

Iskendar will fall, again

They were repeating even in the recesses of her thoughts when the monster had gone, dragging back into the distance.

Iskendar will fall, again

When she had long left the school and made it home to warm greetings from her family.

Iskendar will fall, again

Alone back in her room, she found she could block it out, but it required the usual distraction she used. She started studying. Seeking an answer. When she stopped thinking at all,

Iskendar will fall, again

was there.

CHAPTER TWENTY-SIX

Quint crashed through the garden gate, a look of horror on his face. He stumbled several steps forward, then let go of the gate. Too surprised to speak, Hypatia and Aurelia looked on. He took another step and collapsed forward, limp as a ragdoll, into the patch of flowers in front of him. He landed hard enough to send clumps of dirt splashing into the reflecting pool.

Hypatia and her mother leapt up, shouting at the same time.

"Dad!"

"Quint!"

Hypatia was the first to reach him, turning him over while Aurelia brushed the dirt from his face and clothes. He groaned in pain. The dirt stuck to Aurelia's hands and she was wiping it on her dress. Hypatia stared at its skirt for a beat. "Mother . . ."

Aurelia looked down at her dress. The cloth was smeared red. "Is this blood?" She looked back at Quint. "He's cut. Find it."

Frantically they checked his arms and legs. "Did he hit something as he fell?" Hypatia wondered.

"No, his shirt is ripped, here, under the coat." Aurelia's hand quickly skimmed the length of the tear; evaluating the severity of the damage it was hiding. "It's serious. Really bad." She sounded scared. "Lay him down on the bench."

Hypatia lifted him under his arms and her mother grabbed his legs. It took considerable effort to move him, especially with her mother torn between moving Quint and running for help. He groaned again as they both lowered him to the bench.

"Dad, I am so sorry," Hypatia apologized helplessly.

Aurelia pulled aside his coat and pushed up the shirt. The cut, now clearly more of a ragged gash, was deep enough that the yellow fat was visible in the folds of it. Blood pulsed out and spilled over the white stone.

He coughed and tried to speak. Aurelia attempted to soothe him and grabbed a pillow that had been knocked off the bench to apply to the wound; he cried out again. Hypatia gripped his hand.

He drew in a deep, distressed breath. "The Library, stay—" A coughing fit overtook him and his back arched in spasm.

"Hold this." Hypatia's mother grabbed Hypatia's free hand and used it to apply pressure to the pillow turned bandage. "I'll get the medical kit."

Hypatia held the pillow in place with as much pressure as she could apply, barely containing the flow of blood, which was now pooling on the ground. Her other hand was still in the grip of her father's pale fingers.

"The Library," he started again, and Hypatia attempted to soothe him as her mother had done moments before.

"Relax, Dad. Don't worry about the Library now." She was whispering because it seemed more calming to talk to him at that level. "I will check on the Library soon enough."

"No!" he shouted, and blood sprayed from his mouth. "Stay away." He convulsed sharply as he spat out each word.

"Why?" she exclaimed in alarm. Whatever had done this was at the Library, and there would be many people in that district at this time of day.

"Monster . . . shadows . . ." His gaze was drifting off. He muttered other words Hypatia was unable to make out.

Her mother returned with the kit. She pulled the pillow away. Fresh blood shot from the wound, but Aurelia was prepared, applying cloths and medical tape for pressure. She also cleaned and protected the wound as expertly as could be managed in a garden.

"He said something about the Library."

"Don't worry about that now." Her mother had become cold and serious. "Once I have this covered we need to get him inside. Then you need to get the doctor."

Hypatia nodded and they worked together silently; when Aurelia was done they dusted the rest of him off and carried him as gently and smoothly as they could into the living room to deposit him on the couch.

"The bed would be better, but we'd undo all our work if we tried to move him so far." Aurelia faced Hypatia after a final check of their handiwork. "Go get the doctor now."

Hypatia took off in a burst of adrenaline. She was through the garden and out the gate before she could piece together a thought about what she was doing or where she was going. She stopped to think and in the sudden quiet, she could hear herself breathing: shallow, laboured, and wet. She

126

wiped away tears that had appeared without her noticing.

"This is all on me," she said quietly. Her legs wobbled and wet sobs replaced her shallow breathing. Her legs crumpled beneath her and Hypatia dropped to her knees, weeping openly. Her hands slammed into the dirt and she bowed her head to bury her cries in her own breast, to hide her shame. It was a reckoning Hypatia had known would come. Maybe it wasn't at her hand directly, as she thought it would be, but the rocks were loosed by her actions. Now the landslide was falling on her world. Her father. Her sobbing continued until she ran out of breath to sustain it. She sat silently, looking as if she were in prayer. The wind brushed against her and made her tear-soaked skin feel cold. She heard voices on the breeze.

"Jet?" she said hopefully.

There was no reply.

"I need you," she added, trying to hold back another wave of guilt.

The voices grew louder. They weren't a man's voice or even the sounds of someone wrighting. They were screams. Shouts, cries for help, all panicked; they were distant but getting clearer and closer.

Looking up toward the Capital, Hypatia noticed smoke streaming up from several districts. The ribbons of blackness contrasted starkly against the pink sky of a setting sun. The largest plumes were drifting up from the district around the Library.

Hypatia scrambled to her feet, a new panic rushing in, flooding out the shame and guilt. Her city was burning. She had to stop it. *But how?* she thought. *What do I do first?*

The doctor.

She ran away from the city.

The doctor had a garden of renown, thick with trees, innumerable trellises with cascading vines, and the brightest flowers in the coldest of seasons. Hypatia blew past it all, focused on a singular purpose: *Get help.*

Without a thought for privacy or propriety, Hypatia bust through the front door. "Doctor! Doctor?"

The doctor, seated just inside the door, leapt up in shock. "Yes!" he shouted..

"Fa—" Her attempt came out as a rasping wheeze and Hypatia had to stop to catch her breath.

"Take you time. Do you need a drink?"

"No," was all she could manage, fiercely shaking her head.

"No drink? No time?" the doctor asked loudly, alarmed. "You're covered in dirt, Hypatia."

"My father," she finally got out. "Help."

"Let's go." Given his purpose, he led the way to the door and grabbed a large medical bag on the way out.

They hurried through the garden to the road, but then Hypatia had to grab him by the collar and drag him forward. He'd stopped, wordlessly opening and closing his mouth as he started at the clouds of smoke looming over the Capital. Even in the short time it had taken to get the doctor, Hypatia noticed it had increased significantly.

"Quint needs you now," she said, urging him forward. "The city will need you next."

They ran the distance back to Hypatia's home.

"The city's burning," Hypatia told her mother, watching the doctor work on Quint, who had passed out completely, his breathing laboured. Her mother didn't seem to hear her. Her calm, nurse-like, professionalism was cracking. Fear for her husband's life was creeping in.

"It's a mess," the doctor muttered, referring to the bloody slash.

"I have to go help, Mom."

"No," her mother said.

"I can't let those people—" Hypatia started to argue.

"You heard your father." Hypatia thought her mother had been out of earshot. "Stay. Away."

Guilt settled in her chest and kicked her in the gut. Her crushing responsibility to resolve this made her blurt, "This is all my fault! I have to—" she sought the words for the next action she was going to take "—do something." She was lost without a plan. Tears came again.

Her mother grabbed her in a forceful embrace. Speaking directly into her ear, she said in a voice that was half pleading, half shaken, "This is not on you. We make choices. You made choices that were innocent and you thought were right. You aren't responsible for the storm because you asked for rain." Looking Hypatia in the eyes, she added, "Strangers came to Iskendar. They brought this."

She pushed her mother away at this. "Jet? You blame Jet for this?"

"Yes, Hypatia, I do."

"You haven't seen what I have. You know nothing. Jet is kind, responsible." She thought of their time on Regen. He had taken care of her, been so close and so loving. Memories flooded in—the monster, Arcadia falling, and how he'd wrighted them out at the last moment. "He saved me."

"Before Jet," Aurelia spat his name with a ferocity that scared Hypatia, "everything was perfect."

The Catalogue took over, and Hypatia became focused, cold, and direct. "Mother, you may blame Jet and, as you do, hold me responsible for it as well. His fault is mine as mine is to be his." Her boldness made Aurelia take a step back. "I am going."

The Catalogue strode out the door.

Aurelia called after her. Her mother would have forcibly brought Hypatia back into their home, confined her and kept her safe. Yet this was the future Great Librarian that Iskendar had chosen, not the scared child. Walking briskly, nearly marching, she headed toward the Capital.

She fought the desire to run, knowing that if she let the dread and the panic in she would not be as calculating, as emotionless and effective as The Catalogue could be. It was time to earn her place in history and no one, not even her mother, was going to stop it.

A plan was forming as she passed the café and a woman with two children ran past, away from the city, paying no attention to Hypatia. She saw the fear and hopelessness on the woman's face, and forgave her. Few others were running from the city. It was the civic duty of all citizens of Iskendar to help. Logic would, ultimately, trump fear.

It was the reason many would not flee. *The reason why many will die, too,* she thought. Blame bubbled in her throat and Hypatia allowed her pace to quicken in response as she physically swallowed back the emotion.

At the intersection where the road branched off in the direction of the Library, which had been her planned destination, she heard shouts coming from the opposite street—war cries mixed with screams of pain. She followed them to a crowd of people in the next block. They stood in a circle, many of them wielding improvised weapons: stones, clubs, knives, and other everyday objects. They were surrounding something. Hypatia pushed her way through the crowd to find out what it was.

In the open area in the centre of the crowd stood a skeletal black figure. It was almost a shadow of a nightmarish monster. It held a black sword in one hand and the limp body of a person in the other. Flinging the body clear over the throng of people, it lashed out with the sword. A group of students, bolder than most others and younger than Hypatia, managed to avoid the swinging blade. A woman, a stately figure she recognized from parliament, was not so agile. The sword connected and she was sent sprawling, the club she was carrying flying from her hand to strike another man toward the back of the circle. She crumpled into a heap where she landed, unmoving.

Someone shouted, "It can't be stopped. You need to run."

Another voice: "No, it will ruin the Capital. We fight it here. *Now!* Before anyone else gets hurt."

Pleas of helplessness met with cries of anger. This was followed by a call to attack, and the group surged forward.

Hypatia was pushed behind the crowd as it happened. Stumbling, she grabbed a stranger for both balance and answers. "What happened?"

The man, an aged cabinet minister whom she recalled talking with at her inauguration so long before, shakily replied, "It came from the Library."

Hypatia let go of the man and strode off toward the Library as a cheer of success erupted from the crowd. She turned around in time to see a red flash. After a moment's silence, another cheer rose from the crowd. Determined, she turned back to the Library.

A fire was blazing, ashes spewing out and sparks bursting occasionally, but the Library wasn't the source of it, Hypatia discovered. A storehouse of goods—fuel and other essentials—was engulfed in flames. A gout of fire exploded outward from it as Hypatia ascended the stairs to the Library. She could feel the heat of it from the other side of the square. The space between her and the fire was littered with torn clothing, crumbled stone, books, and papers. One of the Library's ancient doors was open and the other was missing entirely.

She leapt down the inner stairs three at a time and paused at the bottom of the staircase, surprised by how out of breath she was. Her confident pace faltered as she stepped toward the table, intent on the forbidden portion of the Library on its far side.

Someone shoved her from behind and she stumbled into the table. She tried to turn but she was shoved again and, already off balance, hit the floor, landing on her shoulder so hard she heard the humerus grind in its socket. She rolled to her chest to take the weight from her shoulder, hoping to reduce the pain.

A foot pressed down on her back.

"Everyone thought you were the future." It was Kalli's voice, but with a guttural anger that didn't fit the Librarian's fragile frame. "But he comes."

For some reason Hypatia though Kalli meant Jet, and pictured him throwing Kalli off her back and scooping her from the floor in rescue.

"The Kek will use your fear to enter. He will infect your mind."

Clearly, Hypatia thought, struggling against Kalli's foot, they weren't thinking about the same he. "Let me up. I need the archive. The answer is there. The Founders—"

"The Founders," Kalli cut in, "hid the Kek from us. To save us."

Hypatia tried to push herself up but her shoulder screamed in agony, and she shuddered. In reaction Kalli pressed harder with her foot and shifted the pressure toward the injured limb.

"The *Arcadia* failed. They will all fail."

"The archive will have the solution."

"There is no archive."

Hypatia stopped struggling. "No archive?" *How could there be no archive,* she thought, thrown into confusion over what she knew or what she had known. *We've always been taught of the Founders' archive.*

"Only the tablet, the light of the Founders knows all. It knows of the Kek, of the Founders' journey, and of their rules for Iskendar. It is a story of failure."

"Give it to me." She reacted quickly, rolling to put Kalli off balance. The Librarian over-extended her leg and stumbled. Hypatia flipped to her back and shuffled away from the woman.

Kalli's eyes were sunken and dark, with bags of puffy, bruised-looking skin under them. Pulling back thin lips to sneer at Hypatia, she spoke again in the sinister, unnatural tone she had greeted her with. "It is dead."

"How can a book be dead?"

"It is not a book. The tablet is a repository of knowledge. Forbidden as the technology it resides within."

"How is that possible?" Hypatia asked, but as the words left her mouth, she understood. *The Founders had the technology to bring them to Iskendar; of course they would have something more advanced than books to store information.*

"It matters not, because it is dead," Kalli said in an emotionless voice. "And it matters even less because the Kek are already here. Soon we will all be dead too."

"What did the archive say? How do we stop them?" she shouted desperately at Kalli.

"It said we could run. We can hide. Bury our knowledge and bury the Kek." She sneered again, the dark side of her returning. "But that doesn't work. They know how to dig and climb into our minds to make flesh of themselves. They control the chaos and breathe life into it."

"If they breathe life, why is there so much death?" She thought of Jet's home, of Meeko, Regen, their Arcadia and the people outside. "The Founders were protecting us from this. The fate they sought to avoid is upon us."

"The Founders sought only to delay it. It was and will always be inevitable."

"Does the tablet say all this?"

"Some." Kalli thought on this, her tone and demeanour switching rapidly between thoughtful and dark. "Though the age of it is much greater than they even perceived."

"What does that mean? How would you know more than the Founders?"

Paying no attention to Hypatia's additional questions, the Librarian continued. "It is a cycle. Eons between the risings. We are always beaten. We will be beaten again."

"You make no sense, Kalli. How can we be beaten before the battle? Just now, outside, a crowd took down one of those . . ." She paused to think of the right word.

"Kek," Kalli said. "Call them what they are. The victory is small. An arrow strikes at the scout of a battalion. A rock broken will not move the mountain."

"What is the mountain, then? The Kek?"

"It is much more. The Kek is chaos made form. Nightmares given purchase in reality."

"If the cycle always comes, how do we stop them?"

"You aren't listening, child. We are beaten already. Every rise precedes a fall. We rebuild and chaos follows. Sooner or later it finds us."

"If there is a way to rebuild there must be survivors." She had found her feet and was keeping her distance from Kalli in what must look like a strange, slow dance around the table.

Kalli laughed as if Hypatia had made a joke. "The Founders were allowed to leave. They made plans to rebuild and keep the chaos at bay so humanity could have an eon of peace. For Geb commanded it."

Hypatia had never heard that word spoken aloud. She had never said it, even in the quietest or most isolated study. Hearing Kalli say the name lent some power Hypatia could feel. "Did they tell you?"

"Say it, Hypatia. I know in all those texts floating in your brain, Geb is there. The Kek are coming through." Her words drifted from her mouth in wisps of white smoke.

"Kalli, what have you done?"

"The Kek are coming, Hypatia. We are the fate through which it wrights." The smoke started to take form, coalescing into another skeletal figure. A jagged sword was taking shape.

"You are more valuable than this old woman." The voice came from Kalli, but was not her own. It was higher; it sounded like her own voice had been twisted and stretched thin.

Before reaching full form, the skeleton pulled back its sword and buried it into Kalli's chest. The sound of the ridged blade scraping her ribs and cracking them was sickening. Kalli slumped to the floor and the tablet fell from her coat.

It glowed in the low light of the Library.

Perhaps it isn't dead, she thought. *It would have the answers. The Founders knew how to fight the Kek.*

The skeleton pulled its blade free and started toward her.

She expected it to shamble and was surprised as it leapt with one foot extended, catching her in the chest. She fell to the floor again. It stepped on her stomach and she could feel the blade lightly pressing on her neck. She closed her eyes.

There was an audible thud and a cracking noise and Hypatia felt the weight of the creature lift off. Another cracking sound was followed by something wet hitting the stone floor. More wet smashing, swinging, tearing, and heavy breathing.

"Aeych!" The voice was soft but firm.

"Jet?"

"Aeych, we have to go."

She opened her eyes but some viscous fluid blurred her vision. She tried to wipe it away.

Jet lifted her, steadied her on her feet, and cleaned her face off. "Are you hurt?"

"I don't think I am." She could make out his figure now; with most of the goo cleared off, her sight was returning. "I thought you—"

"If you aren't hurt, we need to run."

"You—" she stammered. Her heart fluttered.

"No time now." He grabbed her hand and turned to run.

She stood her ground as he was turning and pulled him in before he could take a step. As he whipped back toward her, Hypatia grabbed the back of his neck and yanked his face to hers. It was a rough way to kiss him but he sank into it. His other hand was on her back and he was kissing her too.

All the tension, fear, stress, loneliness, and sadness of weeks alone bled away instantly. Each moment of the kiss was equal to the time they had been apart.

Iskendar was burning a world away.

Jet pulled his face back slightly. "Ah . . . wow."

Her hand still on his neck, she turned his head to whisper in his ear, "Now we fight." She bent down and picked up the tablet.

The screen was cracked. The light still shone from it, but the words were unreadable.

CHAPTER TWENTY-SEVEN

"The answers were here." Her voice sounded strained as she tried to reason with the broken device. "How do we find the answers—what the Founders left us?"

"There is no prophecy, Aeych." His hand was on her head, holding her close, nose pressed to his cheek. "No storybook hero to save us," he whispered. "Worlds have been lost. So many more will fall."

She tried pushing him away. "How is this helping?" Tears were streaming down her face and the tablet slipped from her hand.

"Because you can stop it."

She laughed, sounding almost maniacal with panic. "Me?"

"You, me. All of us."

He had been gone. Hypatia knew in her heart it was forever. She had given up hope, ready to resign herself to a life she had built. Stable. Determined. Solid as stone. But here he was again, hands in her hair, keeping her focused on his eyes. Then he pivoted away to stand at her side.

He had brought others with him.

A dark-haired woman stood a short distance away. She was equal to Hypatia in height but more muscular, wearing what Hypatia thought must be leather armour that accentuated her excellent fitness. A wiry blond man, in similar but less flattering armour, kept watch through the big window. A hulk of a man easily two feet taller than Hypatia leaned against a bookshelf. He appeared to be stretching his calves. He stopped when he noticed Hypatia looking at him and picked up a huge metal club.

Jet spoke before Hypatia could say anything. "This is Sessca." The woman nodded. "The big guy is Bastion."

The smaller man stepped in front of Bastion. "Denys." He raised a hand

WRIGHT

as he introduced himself.

Jet added, "They're gatewrights. Fighters."

Hypatia paid little attention to them. She looked to Jet, fear consuming her. *Four fighters against a world of darkness*, she thought. *We don't stand a chance.*

He was staring back at her. *Those eyes*, she thought. *A blue ocean that calls to be crossed. A typhoon, reckless, crazy, and free.* Everything Hypatia wanted was out there. She saw her future in the chaos of the storm.

"No," she blurted. Through a cascade of tears, she gurgled it again: "No."

"No?"

"No, not us. Not you or them." She pulled away and looked him in the eyes. "Me."

Jet opened his mouth to speak, to refute her argument, but Hypatia cut him off. "It's all here, in the Library. The answers."

"We don't have time to look in all the books for answers."

She smiled, her eyes shut. "It's all stored, organized, and Catalogued. We don't have to."

"You already have."

"I already have," she said at the same time, then kissed him. Hypatia opened her eyes and the restless ocean of blue changed from chaos to determination. Hypatia knew it was because he saw that same look from her.

"I'll need you and the others for this, though. Get behind me and" — she spoke directly to Bastion— "weapons ready." He smiled at her. She was moving before the sentence was done, heading toward the stairs.

"Wrights! Time to go." The remaining gatewrights reacted to Jet's command. "Behind me. Be ready."

"What's the plan?" the wiry gatewright, Denys, asked.

"Do what Aeych says."

"But—"

"Without question. Without hesitation. Trust me. Trust Hypatia."

"Not a problem," Sessca chimed in quickly.

The smaller man quieted and fell in line behind the others.

They emerged from the Library, thrusting the lone wooden door wide. Jet had caught up with Hypatia and was by her side as they descended the stairs into the crumbling courtyard. A black silhouette, nearly four feet in height, was prowling near a grand fountain. It moved like a goat on two feet, awkward and unnatural. A foot-long horn protruded from its head.

"It's a karakadon." Hypatia pointed at it as she spoke. "From the legends of Faunus." It turned on them and charged. "Strike the horn! It's the weak point!"

135

The karakadon silhouette leapt at Hypatia and Jet cut it down at the horn as it reached her. She didn't flinch. The horn shattered into pieces that burned and disappeared before they hit the ground. The beast landed hard on the stone in front of her. A crackling noise, like the sound of an open wood fire, emanated from its body. There was a scream as it reached a breaking point and shattered in a brilliant, bright red flash of light.

Jet covered his eyes instinctively. By the time he opened them again, Hypatia was on the move. *It isn't Hypatia*, he thought, *it's The Catalogue.*

The rest of the gatewrights stared at where the karakadon had just been, speechless. They snapped out of it at Hypatia's shout.

"Another. Same weakness."

Jet was dispatching it as a large monster thundered around the corner.

"Hobgoblin. Go for the stomach," came the call from Hypatia.

"Got it," shouted Sessca as she ran at it.

Dodging a slow, arcing blow from the log-sized arms of the silhouette, Sessca got behind it; a massive fist drove a crack into the stone walkway. Sessca swung for the back.

"I said stomach!" Hypatia shouted.

As the sword connected, the hobgoblin shape leaned sideways, grabbing the wound and leaving its stomach exposed. Sessca slid under the hobgoblin's arm and struck a second blow, this time into the stomach.

A crunch. Crackling. A scream. Swallowed up in a blinding flash of red light, it vanished.

As the smoke cleared Sessca said, "I heard you the first time."

CHAPTER TWENTY EIGHT

Gaius crouched under the desk. The noises of people retreating sounded distant and disconnected from the fear he was feeling. The smell, a stench of rotten bogs and smoke, kept him in the moment. It kept Gaius afraid.

Being brave on Iskendar was about voicing an unpopular idea, getting up in front of the smartest people in the city and telling them they were wrong. Or, in Gaius's case, standing up in front of the woman who was everything to you and professing your desire. Telling her "I love you" when it could end the friendship and ruin any future. That was brave on Iskendar.

"And look how well I did with that." He laughed nervously and heard it echo in the dark.

This is death for everyone, he thought, *but when this home falls, Jet will save Hypatia.* Moments before he had seen Jet rushing up to the Library with a group of strangers he knew must be from another world. *Heroes. All of them.* He imagined the others being welcomed home to their— *Where are they from?* he thought. Welcomed home in a heroes' parade. Smiles on their faces, waving from animal-drawn carts. Each hero on their own float, in his mind, marked with the number of kills. Showered with cheers and gifts and—

Shouts from Hypatia broke his concentration.

The shouting was too far away from him to make out what she was saying. Names? Commands? He recognized The Catalogue immediately without hearing the words. The tone was clear enough. In his excitement, he sat up quickly. His head connected with the desk, hard enough that his vision went white for a moment. When he recovered his senses Gaius slid out and rushed to the nearest window, rubbing his head.

He saw something bursting into a bright light and the others tearing off down the street toward his café. Finding the door, he ran out into the road and was bombarded with the odours of mold, sulphur, and rot along with the smell of the burning city.

Screams and cries in the distance swirled into the courtyard and echoed so much, Gaius could not tell where they originated. The air around him was whipping with an electricity that made the nerves in his arms tingle. He stood paralyzed by the intensity of it all for a moment. Fear tried to take him over.

Another call from The Catalogue and he reacted by bolting in her direction from a stumbling start, still dizzy. His legs gave out and he collapsed to the street. Gaius tried to break his fall with his hands, but it was too late and he took a stone curb on the jaw. For the second time in a few minutes, the world went white.

CHAPTER TWENTY-NINE

Hypatia leapt over the low wall that marked the café's boundary in a graceful sweeping motion.

Jet shouted, "We don't have time for drinks!"

"I'm looking for Gaius." She pushed past the bistro tables and started calling, "Gaius, we have to go!" A sound of furniture breaking and wood hitting walls came from inside.

"I don't think that's him, Aeych."

The crashing grew louder. Pots and glasses were being smashed in a discordant clatter.

The wooden door of the café started to swell, straining against some heavy weight behind it, threatening to blow apart.

"Back away, Aeych. We'll get this." Jet signaled to the largest gatewright. "Bastion, get behind me. I'm going to pop this keg."

He grabbed the handle and looked back at Bastion, who nodded. With one canne clutched tightly in his hand, he yanked the door handle with his other hand. Instead of opening the door, he ripped the handle off and fell onto his back. The door was still in place.

"Maybe try turning the handle," Bastion suggested sarcastically.

"Yeah, thanks," Jet said, dusting himself off and casting the broken handle aside.

As the words left his mouth, a deafening crash preceded splintering wood, followed by a hellish scream. A tall, thin black shape flew from the doorway. It had four legs and a multitude of long tails thrashing wildly behind it. It landed squarely on Jet, who had risen to a crouch. With a grunt he fell back again, this time with the monster on top of him. The beast opened its barbed mouth to consume its prey. Jet swept out his hands with blinding speed, managing to grab a piece of the splintered door and drive it into the creature's mouth.

Bastion jumped forward to strike, but the monster anticipated the attack and struck him in mid-air with a lashing tail. The large man spun away, tumbled to the ground, and slid under a table. Chairs scattered as he connected with it.

"Aeych!" Jet shouted. He was losing the strength contest between his door fragment and the sawing jaws of the creature. "Ideas? Now, please!"

"I don't know, Jet. I've never seen one of these before."

"Any similarities?"

"It has limbs; maybe aim for those."

Denys charged in swinging and was cast back into his own table by a tail.

Another tail ripped a piece from remnants of the café door and launched it at Sessca. She swung to deflect it but was thrown off balance. A second chunk followed and connected fully, driving her back into the already collapsed Denys.

Jet took advantage of the weight shift the thing had to make for the throw, kicking out one of its legs. The monster tilted backward and Jet leaned into the move, rolling up and over the beast as it fell. "Run!" he shouted just before he landed with a grunt and spilled into more furniture.

He tried to crawl out of the mess but a curved claw ground into his calf. He instinctively swiped at it with his weapon and a whip-like tail smashed it away. It dragged him out from under the table Jet was attempting to pull down for cover and snarled something guttural, raising the free claw in preparation for another strike.

A song was being sung somewhere. It was too quiet for Jet to understand the words, but loud enough he could make out the melody. He glanced in that direction, despite knowing that turning away from the beast would quickly end his life.

Gaius stood at the edge of the café, behind the low wall that marked the border of the patio. He didn't look like he was faring well; blood matted his hair and covered half his face. Jet couldn't help but find the whole situation strange as this bloodied man, hands clasped in front of him, sang. He sang in a language Jet couldn't understand, but the melody and tone made it easy to understand the intention of the music. It was a funeral hymn. It was reminiscent of something Jet had heard many times before.

The pain in his leg spiked as the claw withdrew. Jet looked up. The monster was swaying in time with the hymn.

Gaius pointed at Sessca and then back at the rapt creature. He made a chopping motion to his own forehead. Sessca grabbed a broken cup and looked back at Gaius, who was now holding up four fingers. He immediately dropped one.

The song was reaching a crescendo.

Sessca nodded, clearly understanding what Gaius meant.

He dropped another finger and the monster stretched out a neck too long for the stocky body. The music rose as Gaius sang passionately of sadness and loss and hope intertwined.

"How beautiful," Hypatia said in an awed voice, somewhere behind Jet. "I didn't even know he could sing."

Two fingers remained. Gaius dropped another.

Jet slid out from under the creature but stayed close for fear he would distract the thing from its strange reverie if he scrambled away.

The song slipped into a final sad note and the beast lowered its head as if in prayer.

Gaius closed his fist.

Sessca struck it in the temple with the sharp ceramic shard. It screamed and fell in front of Jet. Sessca pulled back the shard to strike again, but there was no need; the outline of it flashed quickly in red fire and vanished. She threw the cup at the place where it had been for good measure and it shattered.

"What was that thing?" Hypatia said to Gaius, who was swaying woozily. She didn't know who to attend to, with Jet bleeding out on the patio and Gaius nearly falling over by the café wall.

"A colngawny," Gaius replied.

"I have never heard of them."

Gaius smirked. "The colngawny is a legend from the coffee fields of Trieste. It was believed that he protected the small creatures that fed off the plants, driving away farmers. The leaf-pickers sing together as they work to ward it off." He sat down on the stone wall and put a hand up to check his head wound. "The fable says he was killed by a stroke to the head from a woodsman protecting his wandering child from being stolen away."

Jet was being helped up by Sessca, one arm around her shoulders. "Gaius, you're with us. I won't be singing anything."

Hypatia couldn't help but feel a flush of jealousy, seeing Sessca, in much better shape than her, helping Jet to his feet. She moved to help Gaius, knowing that a part of her did it just in response to Sessca. "Are you okay?" she asked.

"I'm fine," both men replied at the same time. Jet added, not noticing Gaius had answered and that Hypatia was looking away from him, "He hit me pretty good, but I should be alright."

Sessca snorted and Jet looked up at Hypatia.

"I'm okay," Gaius said. "I'm just dizzy, that's all. Hit my head."

141

"Let me clean that up." Hypatia grabbed some cloth napkins from a surprisingly unaffected table and began dabbing at his head.

"Well, at least he's okay," Jet said as he passed out.

CHAPTER THIRTY

"The five of us clearly aren't enough for this." Denys had spoken little since they defeated what he was calling the coffee monster.

They had agreed on a short rest to recover and bandage up Jet. The group had moved inside the shop and spread out amongst the small tables. Bastion and Denys sat at one table. Bastion was ready to go another round as Denys sipped on a cup Gaius had prepared.

Sessca, seated on a stool at the bar, took a cup of coffee from Gaius and sniffed it deeply.

Hypatia was cradling Jet on a bench in the only booth. Jet was awake but very obviously still shaken and Hypatia had been tending him as he came to.

"With the right knowledge and the right tools," Hypatia said to Gaius, "our people could take the fight to the monsters. I saw them do it outside the Library."

"The casualties would be immense," Jet said groggily.

"Maybe, but what choice do we have? They can work together and words spread on Iskendar faster than the breeze can blow."

Gaius, who had been preparing more coffee, added, "We need to tell a lot of people at once. The more ears, the more help spreading the word."

"On Sana we have a meeting place," Sessca said. "Do you have something like that here? We send out a call to meeting with a tolling of the bell."

"The amphitheatre." Gaius was forming an idea. "We need to get the people there. Then you, The Catalogue, give one of your lectures. If we announce it, everyone will come."

"Everyone will come for a lecture?" Denys looked skeptical. "I wouldn't expect a good turnout for that back home."

"On this world, Hypatia is their Matron," Jet said as he started to sit up, "the voice of authority and security. The people love her."

"They did once, but not as much now. A lecture on how to survive will get them together, no matter who holds it." Hypatia pulled Jet back down. "You stay. We need a demonstration and not a lecture, though. Can we get one of those things trapped and brought to the amphitheatre?"

Denys chuckled. "Killing them was hard enough. Capture seems like it would be ten times more difficult."

Bastion spoke for the first time since she had met him. "We lure one there, sure. Chasing us is something the Kek do well."

"Oh good. Who gets to be the bait?" Denys said.

"That sounds like volunteering," Sessca replied, smiling as she took a drink from her coffee. It was steaming hot but she didn't flinch as it went down.

Hypatia spoke. "Gaius and I will have to spread the word of the demonstration. I'll go downtown with Jet and herald. Gaius, you take Sessca and cover as much of the suburbs as you can. The amphitheatre is five blocks behind this café. You can't miss it."

Jet quickly rose from the bench before Hypatia could pull him back down. "We have our orders." He looked out the window and added, "When the moon is at its highest, have the thing in the auditorium. Will that give us long enough to get people there, Aeych?"

"More than enough."

It took half the time Hypatia had expected to gather an audience. She and Jet tore through the streets. He was fast despite the injury to his leg, and people were eager to receive some hope. They recruited many of those they met to tell others and soon people were buzzing with the news.

When they arrived at the amphitheatre, it was packed and lined up out the door. There was loud chatter, crying and shouting, and, to Hypatia's surprise, some laughter. Even in the worst of times there could be mirth.

As those in the doorways saw Hypatia approach, they quieted, the silence rippling back from them. Jet was ready to physically clear a path, but they parted. Hypatia slowed and felt, for the first time since her inauguration, reverence. She was more than a person. She was hope. They passed into the amphitheatre and she saw Gaius and Sessca on the stage, looking in her direction. She waved and made her way quickly down the stairs, leaping up on the stage beside Gaius. The crowd cheered.

Jet followed closely behind her and the cheering burst out again as he took the stage. For him it was a broken and uncertain applause.

As the applause quieted, shouting could be heard from outside.

"Denys," Sessca supplied. "Sounds like he's early."

Bastion burst through the same doorway Hypatia and Jet had entered through moments before and shouted, "He's coming. It's coming too."

Everything went silent. Only Bastion's footfalls could be heard and he descended the stairs.

"You sure he's going to make it?" Hypatia asked.

Jet replied coolly, "If there is one thing Denys is good at, it's running. He will be fine."

The shouting, faint at first, got louder. The words became clearer.

"Merde! Merde! Merde!" Denys ran into the auditorium and crashed into the first row of chairs he encountered, knocking down several people. He spun to look out the door, then he looked upwards. "Sorry about this. I meant to get a small one."

Bastion chimed in, "Yeah, and it flies, too."

As he said this a dark shadow passed high over the auditorium, accompanied by the whoosh of a large set of beating wings. Moments later, a blast of air rushed downward. Those gathered in the amphitheatre looked around, visibly shaken.

It circled the amphitheatre at an immense height, gliding on unseen drafts as if it were hanging in place on strings. Despite a lack of obvious eyes, Hypatia could tell it was glaring down at the assembly, seeking prey. It circled in ever tighter and lower turns.

There were very few creatures on Iskendar capable of flight that were larger than a finch, so the people were awed by this monstrosity apparently defying the laws of gravity.

It drew close enough, passing below the tops of the columns that lined the outer walls, for Hypatia to judge the full size of it. It was easily twice as long as a person and quadruple that in wingspan. It twitched, snapped a claw down, shuddered, and then vanished.

Everyone gasped and began looking around with wild eyes to see where it had gone. Strained voices and cries filled the amphitheatre.

As suddenly as it had vanished, it flashed back into existence, much higher up. It was no longer gliding, but hurtling downward in a high speed dive, its wide, jagged beak opening.

Jet was on the move. He leapt from the stage and charged toward the point where the bird would strike. A small man cowered there, paralyzed by the sight of violent death diving toward him. He attempted to gather his robes as those around him scattered. Jet was clearing rows two at a time, landing on empty seats and pushing off people who cried out in surprise, their focus drawn from the monster.

He isn't going to make it, Hypatia thought.

He drew his canne and threw it at the monster as it rotated, pulling its mouth upward and pushing its claws forward. The claws tore at the man's robes and arms as he threw them up in defence. The weapon struck its side, throwing it off balance and knocking it and the terrified man into the aisle.

The monster could not stop its momentum and crashed into a pair of empty seats. It struggled to find footing before pushing off with giant wings flapping, air gusting in their down-sweep. It shuddered, kicked one leg out awkwardly, then disappeared. Jet's second canne passed through the space where it had been a moment before and clattered to the ground.

"I think it hurt a leg," shouted someone from the audience. "Maybe it won't be back." They were clearly scared but to Hypatia's surprise, everyone who had been there was still there.

"You've put us in great danger." Several other voices joined this call. The people were descending into panic. Several had already made their way to the exit as others cried in fear.

Hypatia raised her hand. Stoically standing at the front of the stage, she looked out over her people. She didn't speak. She didn't have to. The assembly quieted. Crying stopped. Shouts were cut short and those who had been leaving returned to their seats. As suddenly as they had panicked, they regained their composure and sat focused like eager students ready to learn.

Hypatia took a few moments after everyone had settled before speaking. Lowering her hand, she said, "No. We are a people of logic. We know and we have seen. It will be back."

As if on cue, it reappeared, circling again. Their eyes followed it and Hypatia could tell that fear was creeping back in. She had to bring them back. *Keep speaking to them. Keep their attention.*

"We know the pattern. First it will pick its prey. We use that to win."

Someone from the crowd shouted, "It'll go for whoever is the most afraid."

"And vulnerable," added a woman's voice.

"Someone near the front, start acting afraid!"

"Cower! Be small! Shake about!" More voices shouted suggestions. "Give that person space and make him a clear target."

A petite woman with dark hair in the front row shouted, "Me! Everyone back away." Hypatia recognized her from the Library. She frequented the section that housed legal precedence. The woman hunched over and drew her arms in close. The people around her jumped away in fear of what was to come—or was it acting? Hypatia wasn't sure. It was all happening so fast.

Hypatia looked up at the monster, which was tightening its gliding circles, sensing the woman was a prime target. "It's working!" she announced.

"How do we stop it?" Jet asked, slowly moving forward, trying to hide any intention of attacking the monster when it swooped in.

146

The audience was quiet. They were all working on ideas. Only the shuffling of chairs and some muffled whimpers disturbed the silence. The creature dipped closer. The woman was shaking violently in fear. The act was becoming reality as her fate floated above her, drawing nearer. Hypatia had her own moment of fear as she considered what would happed to this woman if their plans failed.

The monster crowed loudly, the sound echoing against the walls of the amphitheatre. Everyone looked up at it.

It shuddered, a leg twitched—*The same leg*, Hypatia thought—and then it disappeared.

Most of the people assembled nodded to each other and then closed in on the space where the woman was cowering.

"Jet, the leg! Take the leg!" Hypatia shouted at him.

"Bastion! Knife!" Jet shouted up to the stage. Bastion tossed him one, which he caught easily. It was a utility knife. Small and not for fighting, but Hypatia was confident Jet could make it work. She didn't know enough about flying animals to know how tough their bodies might be.

"Cutting won't work, Jet!" Sessca shouted.

"Trust her. It will," Bastion turned and stated bluntly.

The monster appeared, diving as it had before, but now Jet was the target. He had stepped in front of the woman. The monster, undeterred, continued its dive. The crowd had also closed in around them. They looked ready to pounce.

My people, Hypatia thought. *We can do this.*

Jet stood fast, waiting for the moment. The beak flew upward and the claws shot forward. Jet reacted faster than Hypatia could see, grabbing it above the foot and leaning back. The creature's momentum pulled them both into a spin. Falling to the floor, Jet struggled to maintain a grip on the creature's leg. He pulled it toward him and started sawing with the knife. Those encircling the monster tried to hold it down.

The other gatewrights leapt from the stage, arriving as the monster pushed up and away from the other people who were trying to drag it down. It flapped once, flew upward, and crowed painfully. Then it vanished.

"No!" Hypatia shouted.

"Don't worry." Jet held a leg with a long talon up. "It won't be back again."

CHAPTER THIRTY-ONE

The people had left the amphitheatre confident that their logic would win the day. Jet had briefly described making some defensive tools using garden implements as weapons, and showing his own canne and explaining how they could easily be made.

Gaius offered his café as a base of operations and invited all those in attendance to come there for additional help if it was needed. Hypatia would be there along with the strangers who knew how to fight.

The gatewrights, Gaius, Jet, and Hypatia retired to the café and set up a makeshift base that saw visitors constantly coming in for the rest of the night. As dawn broke, Gaius told Hypatia and Jet to go home and get some rest. He would handle it from there. Gaius had been thinking ahead, training up his own staff to answer the most common of questions and arming them with knowledge of the creatures that had been seen already.

News came in within hours that the Capital had been cleared, and Hypatia finally took that as a cue to rest. Jet had gotten much paler and his wounded leg was hurting him more as the night had gone on.

When they finally made it to Hypatia's home, she quickly checked on Quint and Aurelia, who were sleeping in the living area. Her father had a mild fever but was resting soundly. Aurelia opened her eyes as Hypatia knelt down beside her father. She called her close.

"It's okay, Mom. We're safe."

Aurelia smiled, looked at Jet, then kissed Hypatia once before shooing her away with the instruction to get some rest too.

Hypatia helped Jet to her room and the two of them fell asleep before they had a chance to share a word.

The morning after, fighting ended in and around the Capital. Leaflets

148

were sent out with basic knowledge on how to fight the chaos creatures. Hypatia stayed close to home but welcomed innumerable guests to the garden, providing knowledge whenever some new enemy was discovered. The people had taken on the fight and they were winning.

The gatewrights, when not training others, spent the next few days exploring the sights, smells, and flavours of the Capital and basking in their glory as heroes. Judging by their inability to process the praise, it was obvious that a victory in their war was rare.

Bastion was fond of the food.

Denys was rarely seen and Jet believed he would be travelling, putting distance between himself and the people of the city.

Sessca was fond of something else.

Gaius had never conceived of a future without Hypatia. Interest from other women was nothing new. Beautiful, powerful, and intelligent women had sought his attentions. Gaius had always bored them by showing little interest or only talking about Hypatia.

Something about Sessca's interest lit a fire he was not prepared to deal with. She asked a lot of questions, always curious about the world, the food, and the people; it was as if she was sizing it up. What was new to Gaius was that she also listened and accepted any answer she got. She trusted his word, no matter how vague or short it might be—he was the authority. It was refreshing to be trusted and not have to debate or argue the merits of any ideas, or consider rumours and second-hand information.

The potential for a relationship was distant, he knew that. Sessca was seeking friendly company only. But she would touch him to get his attention or gravitate close to him in social situations. Often she was physically bumping into him when she was in unfamiliar territory. For his part, Gaius appreciated her attention and was realizing that there was room for someone else, an idea he had never considered. Hypatia still held most of his desire and he wasn't willing to completely abandon a future with her yet.

As the days passed it was harder for Gaius to let go of her, seeing how radiant Hypatia was at all of the parties, and there were many. Parties for the heroes. Parties whenever there was a report of success on the outer edges of the Capital. There was even a grand dinner to celebrate how clean the city was after the crews had cleaned. So great was that party that a committee was formed to address the cleanup of the cleanup soiree.

Jet spent most of his time in Hypatia's room, alone or with short visits from Aurelia, who had taken up the mantle of nurse to both Jet and Quint. Hypatia was busy, endlessly meeting to discuss what happened and creating the manual that would be the tool to fight back against the Kek.

Getting sworn in as Great Librarian was a distraction from the important work. Hypatia saw to it that when the request came for her appointment, pen was put to paper that afternoon and it was done without fanfare and without celebration.

The funeral for the last Great Librarian, Kalli, was a massive event that bookmarked the final day of the gatewrights on Iskendar. The events that took place in the Great Library on the final night were known only to the council, Hypatia, and the wrights. During their speeches, Oren and Hypatia lauded Kalli as a hero in her own right. In her own words, Hypatia reflected on how the world needed all the heroes it could get in these dark times.

CHAPTER THIRTY-TWO

Following the service there was a dinner. Following the dinner there was an extravagant social gathering that wouldn't be called a party due to the sombre tone. Hypatia held onto Jet the entire night. He was healed, cleanly dressed, and shaven. She had never thought she would see him in such a tidy state. Secretly she missed her rugged hero. For his part, Jet felt uncomfortable with his appearance and the attention he was receiving.

The night was long but it rushed by too quickly for them. Jet had made it clear there was a place he had to be. Someone he had to get back to. The other gatewrights had made their goodbyes already and left Iskendar after the dinner. The final moments of this night would belong to the two of them.

Hypatia led Jet out of the party and down a hallway. The windows were open and the crisp evening brought in enough cold to raise goosebumps on Hypatia's skin. He held her hand and they walked silently to the Library. She unlocked the doors and they entered together.

As they passed the threshold he took her up in his arms and kissed her with an electricity she hadn't felt in a long time. It was scary and it was exciting. She knew he was leaving now and that he would be back. But this kiss . . .

. . . it might be their last for a long time.

He gripped her with enough force to squeeze the air from her lungs. She squeaked lightly and they both came away laughing. It was nervous and Hypatia could see he was as scared as she was.

"I just want to run, but I can't, Hypatia. I want us to be together again. I think of us lifted on the sails of that ship. Our life together in the skies of Regen. The wind, the constant noise, and the endless thirst. You know,

151

when I need a drink, when I thirst for anything, I think of you."

"Call me Aeych. I love it when you say that name."

"Aeych, these people, your people, they're scared. But you can lead them. I have to leave for a while. I need you to know that it won't be forever. Just for now." She opened her mouth to speak but he looked at her in a way that said her moment would come. "Other people, other worlds need me." He said "worlds," but it was an after-thought; Hypatia sensed he had meant someone specific. "Promise me, when I come back, you can do for other worlds what you have done and will do for Iskendar. Promise me you will always be my oasis, my glass of water, my drop of hope in the chaos."

She smiled slyly, stepped back, and gestured grandly to herself. "Drink it in."

They both laughed but it was bittersweet, heavy with sadness and anxiety.

Grabbing him by the shoulders, she yanked him forward and kissed him hard while moving her hands into his hair. He locked his arms around her, caressed the small of her back.

She could still smell some hint of Regen upon him, as if the dust still clung to his body. Happiness rose in her and she pictured their nights together, struggling to be quiet behind a thin curtain, knowing it was the only privacy they'd find in a room full of people. Not just some people, though. They were a family on that ship.

Meeko.

She was gone.

A tear left her eye and mixed with their kiss.

She pulled back from his lips. "Your sister needs you. You have to go."

Jet looked stunned. "How did you—"

"It was kind of a guess. That confirmed it, though."

"I promise—"

"No more promises. Say hello to her for me." She said this through a last run of tears. "Let her know I look forward to the day we meet." She held him at arm's length.

"I will." There was a look with that response that made Hypatia understand she wasn't exactly right with her guess. Something was off. Jet was troubled.

She dropped her arms and, not wanting to waste more time anticipating the pain of separation, she pulled out his book and untied the cover.

He took it from her, folded it open, and looked up into her eyes.

She stared into his blue sparkling eyes and then bounced forward to kiss him quickly on the lips. She turned and strode back out of the Library, closing the door behind her.

If I don't see him wright I can imagine he never left. That he is still in that room waiting for . . . Her thought trailed off as she heard the sound of pages behind her.

She collapsed, her back to the door, and wept.

It was a short release, sitting there crying. She told herself that it had to be. There was too much work to be done. Wiping away the remaining tears, she checked her dress and strode from the building with determined purpose. *The Guide to Fight the Chaos* would not write itself.

* * *

With all the resources committed to it, the manual was fast-tracked for completion, editing, and publishing. No lengthy approval process was even considered; Hypatia was the sole authority on what was added and what was not. It was rubber-stamped for publication before Hypatia could even finish the first draft.

Thousands contributed and it now took more time to filter suggestions than it did to update the editions. Not only did the number of creatures increase with each draft, so too did the solutions improve. Her days were filled with meetings, discussions, study, review, and interruptions.

Partway through her second draft, she was waist deep in the anthropological study of Azeir-Torel to find the solution for defeating what they called a goddess when there was knock at her makeshift office door. She didn't look up. "Yes?"

"Hypatia?" It was Gaius.

She instinctively pulled her attention from a scroll to see him. She realized how different he looked from the last time she . . . Then it dawned on her. She had not seen Gaius since the night of the attack.

She opened her mouth to speak and he held up his hand. "I'll keep this short."

Hypatia rose, ignoring his gesture and embracing him in a tremendous hug. She could feel his body was tense and she could also feel the tension melt as he wrapped his arms around her. "Gaius, I've been so wrapped up in all this . . ."

"It's okay, Hypatia. I understand better than most what needs to be done. How much this matters to you and to the people."

"But still I should not—"

He cut her off. "Hypatia, I was wrong." She pulled away from their embrace as he continued. "I see not only the way he looks at you but the way you look at him, and I know I've been lying to myself."

He was comparing himself to Jct and she immediately felt her face redden.

"You look at him in a way I've never seen from you and I know . . ." he looked away from her " . . . I know that no matter how much I want it, that can never be me."

"Gaius, I—" She was thankful that Gaius spoke again as she had started speaking, not knowing how she would respond.

"I'm heading to the south. They need someone to help teach the people and represent the Capital."

"They could not have made a better choice. You are the best of what the people of this world have to offer. You are Iskendar." She was excited for him but also worried. "Will you be gone long?"

"We plan for it to take a year, maybe two."

"Oh, Gaius. Is there any way I can stop you?"

"There is, but it would only be selfish of me."

She knew what he meant and did not press further. This was an escape for him from his feelings for her as well as an opportunity to broaden his world. She had heard of his time with Sessca and imagined the kind of impression that would have on him.

"I need you to know, Gaius, that you are my greatest friend. As much family to me as anyone else. You know me better than anyone in this world." She paused. "Better than anyone in this universe." A tear slipped down her face and Gaius wiped it away.

"You come back to me," she begged. "Promise."

"I do."

She saw a tear welling in his own eye and she reached to return the favour, but her turned before she could.

"Thank you, Hypatia. I will see you again."

He left the room before she could say anything else and she understood he did not want her to follow. When she turned back to her desk there was a steaming cup of coffee waiting for her.

* * *

By the fourth draft of the guide, three cycles of the moons had passed and Iskendar had been incident-free for over many nights. The more thorough and complete the guide became, the less frequently the chaos even appeared.

She kept her role as the Great Librarian and further increased the importance her position had in the rule of the Capital and Iskendar. Oren saw his rule strengthened with Hypatia backed as hero by the populace. His trust in her was the catalyst that saved Iskendar, it was said. Others, in isolated circles, still held that the rise of the Assistant to the Great Librarian was the cause and not the cure. The coming of the stranger was also the harbinger of tragedy.

Quint was slow to recover and lost most of his mobility. He spent time in his garden, as he had before, but now he paid workers to tend to all he had built. Acting as a foreman, he was very specific about maintaining it and not allowing any modifications. Only seasons were allowed to hold any sway in his domain.

It hurt Hypatia to see him like this. All the longing she might have for Jet was manageable, knowing he might return any day. Her father, on the other hand, was trapped by his health. The fire drained from his routine. The passion he put into his garden died along with the involvement he once had with friends and family. He was hollowed out, but always put on a brave face for his wife and daughter.

Aurelia would try to raise his interest in new pursuits, but it was obvious he had lost the future he'd envisioned. Peace on Iskendar, planning retirement, and the predictable events of life were lost.

CHAPTER ZERO TWO

Year 222,649 A.L.

Flickering lights on a control panel illuminated a pair of hands in the darkness. The fingers and hands moved spastically over complex controls, slides, and gauges. If there was anyone else watching the lone figure, the way they worked would appear unnatural.

The cloaked figure sat alone at the console. The room was surrounded by dim screens filled with shifting star fields, giving the impression that they were moving quickly through space. The darkness of the universe almost looked darker, despite the dimness of the room. The stars were hiding.

A planet, lush, green, and gigantic, drifted into view. The green light of the planet on the screen illuminated the cloaked face. The colour gave the smile a sickly and unnatural quality.

The figure twitched, then struck a button on the console. All the star fields winked out and were replaced by images of clear capsules that could easily be mistaken as glass coffins, if not for the fact that the occupants, more cloaked figures, were shuffling to life.

Green-tinted lips pulled back, revealing metallic, jagged teeth. The figure turned to the images of the coffins, now all filled with nearly human shapes, smashing on their glass prisons. An alarm sounded and the capsules began to open.

EPILOGUE

"I am alone and he is worlds away."

She bent forward in spasm, gripping the countertop with her nails to keep from falling. She looked up and out the wide framed window at the starless night sky.

The darkness came to her door at night. "But it can't get in," she told herself. "This home, *my* home, keeps me safe." She wasn't referring to the walls or the windows or the doors or the locks of the house.

One hand moved to her belly and she grunted fiercely, her knees nearly buckling. Her other hand dug fingernails deeply into the hardwood counter. The darkness came to her door at night, but not tonight.

Tonight the baby would come.

ABOUT THE AUTHORS

This is the first novel for married authors Stacey and Jason Warren. The world building and romance defining work of WRIGHT is pulled from their unique perspectives including university arts education, working in a noble profession, a ridiculously expansive job history and a passion for all things romantic.

Stacey and Jason live in a sleepy little town in South-Western Ontario with their two awesome children, 1 cat, 2 dogs and are never too far from an adventure breaking out.

For more information on the worlds of WRIGHT or to find out what's coming next for Hypatia and Jet visit GateWrights on the web:

www.gatewrights.com

www.facebook.com/GateWrights/

Made in the USA
Columbia, SC
02 May 2018